Household Obsession

ANYA MERCHANT

Copyright © 2024 Anya Merchant

All rights reserved.

CONTENTS

CHAPTER 1 3

CHAPTER 2 9

CHAPTER 3 12

CHAPTER 4 16

CHAPTER 5 21

CHAPTER 6 25

CHAPTER 7 28

CHAPTER 8 31

CHAPTER 9 37

CHAPTER 10 42

CHAPTER 11 47

CHAPTER 12 53

CHAPTER 13 57

CHAPTER 14 61

CHAPTER 15 65

CHAPTER 16 69

CHAPTER 17 76

CHAPTER 18 80

CHAPTER 19 86

CHAPTER 20 91

CHAPTER 21	99
CHAPTER 22	104
CHAPTER 23	108
CHAPTER 24	113
CHAPTER 25	117
CHAPTER 26	129

ACKNOWLEDGMENTS

Thanks to Zaphod, Numbers, Hayden S., Pygor, Ian S., mm, Yitzhak B., MrKoko, Wolfgang Fugue, and all my other patrons

CHAPTER 1

The house looked much as he remembered, and yet completely different. Jake nodded to the uber driver, feeling both body and mind groaning as he climbed out of the back of the car. He wasn't sure what he'd been expecting after four years, but his arrival felt anticlimactic, regardless.

"I bet they'll be happy to see you," said his driver.

The two of them had made small talk on the way through Pinecross, the usual pleasantries about his destination and plans.

"We'll see," said Jake.

He pulled his suitcase out of the trunk. It felt heavier than the clothes and books and various trinkets he'd acquired over the course of his four years in college, as though it also held the weight of the past he was now returning to. Four years without a single visit home, and now he was back for the indefinite future.

Jake felt the length of those years as he waved the uber driver off and started walking toward the front door, wheeling his suitcase behind him. He hadn't actually brought much with him to school or acquired much extra beyond a game console which he'd kept and a TV which he'd sold. It made him feel oddly vulnerable, as though he were homeless instead of returning home.

He paused at the door and opted to knock instead of just opening it. He was fairly certain it was the first time he'd ever knocked on the door to his childhood home before. Jake waited, letting the wind tousle his hair as he considered that it was entirely possible that no one was there. He hadn't called ahead beyond a single short email he'd sent weeks earlier announcing his intention to return.

He was sure his dad would be away for work, as he always was. His mother Rebecca, well stepmom, technically, would definitely be there. Jaimie, his older stepsister, was two years his senior, making her 23 and liable to have moved out on her own by now. That left Kate, little Katie, his younger stepsister, who would have just turned 18 and be finishing up her last year of high school.

The door swung open. He stared into his mother's face on the other side, feeling a rush of emotions. The one that came out on top was surprise — she looked no different than from when he'd left even though she would now be forty... or forty-one. She was still the same beautiful woman with long, glossy brown hair, affectionate hazel eyes behind trim librarian style glasses.

Rebecca let out a sigh full of emotion and rushed forward to envelop him in a hug. "Oh, Jake, we weren't sure you were coming! I can't believe you knocked — why didn't you just come in?"

"I don't know," he said. "It just feels... so different."

He wrapped his arms around her, grinning despite himself. Different but the same. He felt her body against his, attention shifting to her breasts which he could feel pressed against his chest a little too vividly.

It was still warm for early fall, and Rebecca was dressed for it. She wore a sundress, a yellow thing with white polka dots and thin straps. Jake noted her smooth, lightly tanned shoulders as they broke their embrace, and had to yank his eyes away from lingering where they didn't belong.

"You're home," said his mother. "That's all that matters."

She reached out her hand and cupped his cheek as though he were a five year old instead of a recent college graduate. Jake felt a mixture of amusement and embarrassment.

"Well, I'm here." He grinned and rolled his eyes as his mother began tousling his hair. "You don't have to fawn over me."

"The fawning hasn't even begun yet, mister," she said, smiling back. "I'm still in shock. Even after getting your email, I wasn't sure that you'd actually come back. You missed so many Christmases and Thanksgivings and birthdays."

He shrugged. "I was going to school in another state. It was just too hard for me to make the trip."

He suspected it sounded as lame as an excuse out loud as it did in his head. His mother gave him that look he remembered, the one where it was clear she was seeing right through his bullshit while simultaneously loving him too much to call him out for it.

"Come inside," she said, sliding past him to take his suitcase off the steps.

He felt acutely aware of how close that brought her to him, close enough to give him a faint whiff of her scent.

"I'm going to make you something to eat and you're going to tell me everything."

Footsteps thumped in that all too familiar way from the upstairs hallway that led toward the bedrooms, and a young woman came into view an instant later. She had wavy red hair down to her shoulders, a lithe figure, and a freckled face that only became familiar after a few seconds of churning recognition.

"Katie!" called Jake, with a laugh.

"She insists on Kate now," said his mom, touching his shoulder.

"Katie's fine," said Kate.

Her voice was quiet, and she didn't hold eye contact, only glancing up and around and everywhere but directly at him.

She was dressed in a plaid skirt that barely reached mid-thigh and a white blouse with a red ribbon at the neck - her school uniform, by basic assumption. She looked insanely cute, nothing like the clumsy little sister with braces that he remembered, but still carrying the core of that same essence. She'd always been petite, but there was a softness about her now that made her seem rare and vulnerable.

Jake felt an odd impulse to go over and scoop her up in a bear hug and lift her into the air the way he used to, but he resisted it. She wasn't a little girl anymore. It was both obvious and unfortunate, a fact that might well mean that he needed to discover a new way of knowing her as a person.

"I missed you," he said, opting for raw honesty.

Kate shrugged, but matched him with her reply. "Missed you too."

Jake let out a small chuckle. "You're so quiet now. What happened to the sister I remember who was always stomping around and asking five questions at once?"

Kate glanced away.

His mother winced slightly. "High school. She's still the same old Kate, though."

"Yeah, of course," he said.

He heard another set of footsteps from behind Katie. He recognized Jaimie instantly, though she'd changed nearly as much as Kate had. Her blonde hair was cut short and run through with purple highlights. She had a number of new piercings in each ear along with a spiked metal stud through the corner of her left eyebrow.

Not to mention her tattoos. Her left arm was now a canvas of butterflies and flowers artistically swirled together. It was the type of tattoo that left Jake wondering what other tattoos she might have, along with where they might be. He blinked and realized that Jaimie was watching him stare at her with folded arms.

"Jaimie." He smiled and laughed, again feeling the urge to rush upstairs and hug her. "Wow. I dig the new look."

"I already had a tattoo before you left, for your information," she said, smiling a little despite her tone. "I just never showed it to you."

"Well, they look good on you."

He couldn't stop his eyes from taking in her figure, the tight t-shirt she wore heavily suggestive of her full chest underneath. He did stop quite abruptly as he noticed and realized what he was doing.

"Are you going to review my piercings, too, Jakey-kun?" Jaimie's tone was mocking as she used his old nickname, born from a fascination with anime he'd had as a preteen.

"I'm good." He glanced at his mother again and then slowly began taking off his shoes. "God, this feels so strange. Do I even have a room here, still?"

"Of course you do!" Rebecca pulled him into a smothering hug and kissed him on the cheek. "It's just as you left it."

"Assuming you want to live at home," said Jaimie, moving to lean on the interior balcony banister. "Good luck with that if you intend on getting laid, like, at all."

Jake snorted at the teasing edge in her tone. "You should take your own advice."

"It's different for women, Jakey-kun."

"That's just one of those old, bullshit double standards that don't really exist anymore."

It was Jaimie's turn to laugh. "If that's how you think I feel sorry for the girls you dated in college, assuming you managed to get any dates."

He felt his face flush hot, emotion hitting him as the words echoed out of context. Estelle, his most recent ex, had said something far too much like that. How she didn't see a future for them and felt sorry for herself sometimes for being in a relationship she wasn't happy with.

No, it'd been more brutal than his smoothed over recollection would let him admit. She'd also said bluntly that she didn't see herself ever managing to be happy long term with a man who couldn't make her come.

Asa, his first and only other girlfriend, had always seemed vaguely underwhelmed by sex. She'd taken his virginity, and he'd always wondered if she'd been comparing him to someone else. His face grew hotter.

"Fuck off, Jaimie," he snapped.

Jaimie blinked, mouth falling open slightly. "Well, fuck you too."

"You know, I probably would have looked for my own place if I knew this was how it was going to feel coming back home!"

He snatched up his suitcase and hurried upstairs. Jaimie rolled her eyes and got out of his way. Kate stared past him, seeming detached.

"Jake!" called his mother. "Hold on a second! Jaimie, why did you say that?"

"I was just giving him advice," said Jaimie. "He's the one who told me to fuck off."

Jake seethed as he found the door to his old room and threw it open. There was dust on the knob. He tossed his suitcase in ahead of him and slammed the door.

CHAPTER 2

As far as Jake could tell, his room was exactly as his mom had said — just as he'd left it. He walked over to the bed and sat down, letting himself sink into both the mattress and a moment of stillness. He felt like he needed the latter after his emotional blowup downstairs. He hated how Jaimie always got to him with just a few words, just as she had when they'd been younger.

Though he recognized that she probably hadn't intended to prod him in such a sore place. Part of the reason why he'd finally come home was to get away from Estelle after their breakup. She'd been a junior, and if he'd stayed in town, living in the off-campus room he'd been renting, there would have been far too much of a chance for him to run into her.

He'd also run out of money, with the last of his scholarship drying up, which was also a factor.

He stared at his old computer, now woefully out of date, and the dusty computer monitor atop his desk. There wasn't much more to his room than that, the closet, and his modest twin bed. It was a boy's room, a teenager's room, at best, but it was where he'd be living for the near term. He found it hard to be anything but humble after what he'd been through prior to his graduation and across the past few months with Estelle.

There was a letter on his desk with his name on it, the only thing out of place within the entirety for the space. He recognized his father's handwriting and felt a flutter of anticipation as he grabbed it and tore the envelope open. His hopes blossomed as he wondered if perhaps this was why his mother hadn't mentioned his father, preferring to let the man speak for himself, surprise him in his own way.

Hey Jake,

I'm still stuck out in Christchurch for work. Wish I could have been around to welcome you back. I have leads on some positions for you if you don't mind taking a job that involves remote work. Give me a call when you read this.

Dad

Jake closed his eyes and set the letter aside, feeling his anger welling up again. He wasn't an angry person, but much as Jaimie's words had poked somewhere sore, this letter felt much the same.

His father had always been distant , even in the years before he'd left for college. Part of why Jake had been so steadfast in his refusal to visit had been as a way of cutting back. It felt so prototypical and cliche to attempt to strike at his father by doing what had incensed him in the first place.

He wondered if it had even been striking back, or just a plea for attention in his old man's language.

Jake took out his phone and called his father. It was fairly late in the afternoon, and he knew it would be sometime midmorning in Christchurch. His dad never picked up. He ended the call without leaving a message and flung his phone down on his pillow, so irritated that he began to question his decision to come home in the first place.

"Jake?"

There was a quiet knock at the door. He turned his head to see his younger sister standing in the doorway, Kate now, he supposed.

"Are you okay?"

"I'm fine, Katie. I mean, Kate." He shook his head and let out a small laugh. "I'm not used to calling you that."

"It's fine," said Kate. "You don't have to if you don't want to."

He just looked at her for a moment, struck by how similar and different she seemed from the young girl he'd left behind. He hadn't expected her to come check on him, but she had always done that. She'd been the little sister almost more in tune with his emotions than he was.

But she also seemed so quiet now, so withdrawn, and the effect only became more pronounced as she glanced away from his gaze. He wanted to reach out to her and drag her in for that hug that he'd been imagining downstairs, and then, somehow, pull the past her out of the present one.

"What about you?" he said. "Are you okay?"

Kate shrugged. "I guess."

Jake sighed and patted the bed next to him. Kate gave him a curious look before slowly approaching and taking a seat. She didn't say anything. The old Katie would have been talking his ear off immediately. The old Jake might have only pretended to listen, feigning interest halfheartedly with the tolerance of an older brother.

"Is school going well?" he asked.

Kate gave him a strange look. "Sort of."

"Why sort of?"

She shrugged and didn't elaborate. The mood wasn't right, but not in a broken or worrying way. They just hadn't seen each other in so long. Time away had created new distance to cross, but he would find a way to cross it.

"I think I'm going to take a nap," he said, smiling and touching her shoulder reassuringly. "Tell Mom I'm not going to storm out or anything. I think the plane flight has me a little on edge."

"Okay." Kate stood up, started toward the door, and then turned back around. "I love you Jake."

"I love you too, Katie."

"Do you want me to tell Jaimie that you're sorry?"

"Jaimie can fuck off."

Kate looked stunned. Jake flashed a smile to show her that he wasn't entirely serious and shifted to lay down on his bed.

CHAPTER 3

He wasn't sure how long he'd been asleep when the next knock came at his door. It opened before he could respond or rise out of bed. He turned his head sideways in time to see his mother walking into the room with slow steps, carrying a plate of food and wearing a nightgown. She turned on his desk lamp and he only then noticed how dark it had gotten outside his window.

"I called you down for dinner before, but you were out like a light," she said, smiling. "I fixed you up a plate. Warmed it up just now in the microwave. Chicken stir-fry with rice and frozen eggrolls."

It was his favorite, or it had been before he'd left. He suspected it still was. It'd just been so long since he'd eaten a home cooked meal.

"Thanks, Mom." Jake groaned and tried to summon the effort to sit up. "I'll eat it in a second."

"There's no rush."

Rebecca sat down on the edge of his bed and touched his leg. It was almost like she was keeping a hand on him to confirm that he was still there, that he wouldn't run off like he had before. Her touch was soft and made it surprisingly hard for him to focus, her fingers and palm against his knee over the blanket.

"Jaimie and I always had our banter," he said, preempting what he knew was coming. "If anything, it should reassure you that we're arguing like old times."

"That's not what I'm worried about," said his mom. "Well, not just that."

"I'm listening."

Jake finally managed to push himself up, grabbing the plate from her and taking a bite of the chicken stir-fry. It was delicious. It tasted like home.

"Kate's been having a hard time in high school. Jaimie... well, I suppose you could say she's also been having a hard time, though I think it's more self-inflicted in her case. They both could use a brother in their lives. A brother and a friend."

"Is this one of your therapist suggestions?" he asked, aiming to tease with his tone. "Is there new research showing that mental wellbeing declines in the absence of awesome brothers named Jake?"

"Regardless of whether there is or not, I'm going to need you to be said awesome brother named Jake." Rebecca smirked at him and grabbed his foot. "I could also use my awesome son Jake. We just want you in our lives. I suppose that's what I'm getting at. I don't fully understand why you left and... stayed away for as long as you did."

Jake nodded, knowing it wasn't for a lack of trying. She'd emailed him often, though he'd responded much less so. His mother had gone back to college when he'd been in middle school and converted her career path from teaching yoga and giving massages to being a full-blown therapist. He remembered the shift in her behavior, the way she'd begun to talk about their emotions and fears and beliefs.

"I'm not going anywhere." He set the plate down and looked at her seriously. "Not right away, at least."

His mother smiled warmly and leaned in to plant a kiss on his cheek. It was just a peck, but it sent a flutter of strange emotions through him, more so when he caught the faint scent of her shampoo or conditioner.

"I love you, Jakey." She pulled back, ruffling his hair as her hand slid up from his shoulder.

"I love you too, Mom."

She left his room. Jake ate his food slowly. He got up to brush his teeth once he'd finished, finding the upstairs bathroom much cleaner than he'd remembered it from years earlier. He made an effort to tiptoe back to his room, but found it to be unnecessary.

Jaimie was playing music in her room. He could hear the bass through the wall, a low, rhythmic grumble that seemed to reverberate through his skull. Jake might have been able to simply tune it out if he hadn't taken his earlier nap. The combination of jet lag, the music, and his distorted sleep cycle seemed to promise a night of insomnia.

He fumbled around to find an undershirt, but didn't bother putting his jeans on over his boxers as he made his way out into the hall. The idea came to him to simply go to his mother's room and have her intercede on his behalf, but he tossed it out. It felt too childish, too much like what he would have done as a twelve-year-old.

He knocked on the door of her room, trying to be heard without veering into aggressive pounding territory.

"Yo. Jaimie. Can you turn your music down?"

He waited a few seconds and was beginning to suspect she hadn't heard him when the door swung open. Jaimie stood on the other side in the same tight t-shirt and boy shorts she'd been wearing earlier. Having her so much nearer, however, with him wearing so much less made it seem far more provocative.

"Why should I?" she asked, irritably. "I always play my music this loud."

"I'm sure it was fine back when you weren't sharing a wall with someone else."

"Deal with it." Jaimie jutted her chin out and crossed her arms over her breasts. "This is my house, not yours."

Jake resisted the urge to say something he might regret as the tension simmered and the air suddenly felt hot. He wanted to simply push by her and turn it down himself. He could if he wanted to, being taller and stronger, but it would only spark off more chaos.

"Seriously, Jaimie?" he finally said. "Can't you just—"

"Seriously."

She shut the door in his face. Jake gave in to the urge to bang his fist on it one last time before returning to bed and making another attempt at sleep.

CHAPTER 4

Jake managed to fall asleep eventually. He woke up the next morning and padded downstairs to find breakfast ready and waiting, along with his mother set up with her laptop on the dining room table.

She was already dressed, wearing a gray blouse with a black skirt, light makeup applied underneath her glasses. She looked every bit the part of a therapist in a way that Jake hadn't remembered from before he'd left.

"Morning," she said. "Breakfast is ready. Made some eggs, sausage, and toast with orange juice. Help yourself."

He did so, grabbing a plate and scooping out a sizable serving. He ate for a minute in silence as his mother typed away on her laptop, pausing only to take a sip from her coffee. Kate was next down, wearing her school uniform. Jake hadn't realized just how short the skirt was until he saw her lean forward slightly to grab a piece of toast and it rode up, nearly exposing her panties.

"Morning, Katie."

He shifted his gaze toward his mother, catching the one moment when she was also leaning forward to grab food. Her blouse billowed out and exposed a bit of cleavage, far too much for comfort. Jake cleared his throat as he averted his eyes.

"Morning, Jake," said Kate. She set her plate in front of her and carefully pulled out her chair as she sat down.

"Jaimie isn't joining us?"

Kate shrugged. "I don't know."

"She usually wakes up a little later," said Rebecca. "But I do hear footsteps upstairs."

Jake glanced toward the hallway as Jaimie made her way down. She'd thrown on sweatpants, but her tank top was tight and revealing both in terms of her tattoos and how it hugged her full breasts. He found himself once again unsure of what to do with his eyes. All three of them were gorgeous, and his time away made their beauty seem novel and weirdly intriguing.

"There's coffee too, if you want some," said his mother.

"Absolutely." Jake poured himself a cup and headed to grab the milk from the fridge.

Jaimie was there ahead of him, letting out a tired sigh as she jiggled the jug to see how much milk was left.

"Save me some if it's low," he said.

She glanced at him, finished pouring, and offered him the jug. "Too late."

"Seriously, Jaimie?"

"First come, first serve. Aren't real men supposed to like their coffee black?"

He breathed out slowly and took the jug from her, trying to remind himself that his sister had always had an edge to her, one that only seemed to have sharpened with time. He poured what amounted to a hint of a drop of milk into his coffee and tossed the jug into the recycling.

"Don't fight, you two," said Rebecca. "It's good to have you back Jake."

"Thanks Mom," he said. "I'm trying not to fight, but Jaimie makes it hard."

"Fuck off, Jake." Jaimie rolled her eyes and sat down.

Nobody said anything for a minute. The silence felt conspicuous, not born from Jake's bickering with Jaimie, but the circumstances. He glanced at Kate, who was reading a book next to her plate.

"Do you have to catch the bus, Katie?"

"No," she said.

"I usually drop her off," said his mother. "It suits her better than riding the bus."

Jake raised an eyebrow, but didn't probe further. Jaimie had her phone out and seemed like she wasn't interested in being at the table. He felt like he understood what his mother had meant about his sisters needing a brother and a friend. He also sensed that the act of being said version of himself would take more than a couple of questions over breakfast.

"Speaking of which, we should get moving," said Rebecca. "Ready, Kate?"

Kate nodded and slowly stood up. She smiled at Jake, seeming nervous in a way that made his heart ache for her. She touched his shoulder as she passed by his chair and he caught a whiff of shampoo and the lingering dampness of her hair.

"Don't disappear without checking in with me first," said his mother. She hugged him from behind, arms wrapping around his chest with him still in the chair and kissed his cheek.

"I won't," he said, smiling. "Where would I even go?"

"Some abandoned alleyway with a cardboard box is always an option," muttered Jaimie.

Jake scratched his nose with his middle finger. Jaimie stuck out her tongue at him.

"I'm going to watch some TV," he said.

"Knock yourself out," said Jaimie. "Literally."

He didn't care about the TV, but he suspected staying at the table with just Jaimie wouldn't lead anywhere but toward an argument. The living room was changed in small ways. The TV and the cabinet it sat in were both new. The couch cushions had new covers. It was otherwise the same familiar space, family photos up on the wall and a potted plant sunning by the window.

He searched around for the remote, seeing nothing at first. Knowing his sisters, he assumed it was probably lost in the couch. He lifted the cushions and seemingly confirmed his suspicion. A small remote had been forgotten underneath, but he frowned as he picked it up and examined it.

There was a power button on it, along with an up arrow, a down arrow, a MAX button and a RHYTHM button. He tried power even as he began to suspect that it went to something else. Nothing happened. He flipped it over and read the words on the back.

"Master Pulse...?"

His heart skipped a beat as he realized what he was most likely holding. A remote that worked with something that pulsed, judging by the incredibly specific name. His mind jumped to sex toys, but he slowed himself down. LED lights could pulse. A back massager could pulse.

He felt himself getting strangely excited and had to take a breath and shake his head. He was still adjusting to being home. It was so weird to see both his sisters all grown up. It was almost the same problem, but in reverse with his mother, who seemed suddenly so young and feminine, smaller and lighter than him now that he was a man.

"Are you just going to loaf around the house all day?"

"Jesus!" He flinched in surprise, stuffing the remote into his pocket. "Did you have to sneak up on me like that, Jaimie?"

"Get your hearing checked, dweeb," she said. "But first answer my question."

"No, I'm not," he said, annoyed. "I'll be heading out for a walk as soon as I've taken a shower."

"Good."

Jake stood up and headed for the stairs.

"And save me some hot water!" she called after him.

He said nothing to that, vividly remembering how she'd saved him the milk.

CHAPTER 5

Jake instantly appreciated the shower. His old apartment had been one of the rundown, college town variety, and the water pressure had left much to be desired. Standing under the hot and powerful stream of warmth with steam billowing through the bathroom made him feel relaxed to an extent he hadn't felt in weeks.

He thought about his mother, Katie, and Jaimie. It was so strange to be back and know that he'd be seeing them every day, slotting back into his role as son and brother almost seamlessly. He'd been trying to punish his father by mirroring the distance he kept from their family, but it was clear that the others had missed him, too.

Well, except for Jaimie.

He felt an odd stirring of annoyance and something harder to place as he remembered the way she'd come downstairs in her pajamas and rifled through the fridge with that defiant energy. It felt unfair to call her a bitch even in his head, but he couldn't help but think it. But she was also his sister, who he loved, who he would make an effort to get along with.

He finished his shower, dried off, and went to his room. He needed to do laundry, too, having brought mostly dirty clothing home with him. It took him a few minutes to sort everything out and bring the load to the washer in the basement downstairs. It was only as he was dumping everything in that he remembered the remote in the pocket of his sweatpants and fished it out.

He tossed in the soap and started the cycle before taking another look at his strange find. There was no identifying description on it beyond Master Pulse, written in white and pink, which was suggestive in its own right. Still, the idea that it might go to a vibrator seemed too presumptuous for him to simply accept at face value.

Jake went back up to his room and decided to google the name and model number. He found a website that matched up and stared in blank shock, surprised despite it being exactly as he'd expected. The Master Pulse was a massaging vibrator, though the model description described it as a "powerful passionately pulsating leave-in stimulator" rather than simply a sex toy.

The device itself was small, with a long tail intended for ease of removal. The website promised that it could stimulate a woman's clitoris and g-spot, while also sending powerful pulses to her inner thighs and buttocks.

It had 10 unique intensity settings and was, somewhat obviously, waterproof for use in the bath or shower. There was even a setting for an alarm that would go off if the person with the vibe inserted attempted to take it out without the permission of the person using the remote.

He stopped reading and leaned back in his chair, stunned and silent. He had to acknowledge the facts, regardless of how lurid and conflicting they were. Someone within his household had bought this sex toy. His mother or one of his sisters had bought a leave in vibrator and used it — or had it used on them — at least once, given the remote had been lost in the couch.

He felt himself getting the weirdest, most inappropriate erection of his life. He considered the option of simply closing the browser tab, putting the remote back where he'd found it, and trying to delete the episode from his mind. If only it were that easy. This wasn't something he could forget regardless of whether it would lead to a much healthier outcome.

The worst part was how it seemed like a mocking contrast of his own situation. The vibrator, based off how it was advertised on the website, was closer to something used in BDSM, a dom punishing a sub, rather than even a vanilla sex toy.

His own sex life, in comparison, had been underwhelming to the point of ending his last relationship. It made him feel strange, heated but more in a frustrated sense than in true anger.

The door to his room suddenly banged open. Jake scrambled to close his browser tab and slide the remote out of view. Jaimie took a single step into his room, short blonde hair still wet from the shower. She was wearing a towel and nothing else. Jake tried not to stare at where it tucked into a fold just to the right of her left breast. A bead of water shone in the cleavage of her pale, pinched bosom.

"Asshole," she said. "Did you not hear me when I told you not to use up all the hot water?"

"Have you ever heard of knocking?" Jake stood up and took a step toward his sister. "Besides, I heard you just as clearly as you heard me when I told you to save me some milk."

"There was barely any left," she said, jutting her chin out. "Jerk."

"Crybaby. Go finish your shower."

"Or what?"

He could feel the heat emanating off her body, or at least he thought he could. He found himself wishing that he had the remote in hand, that he could just press the button and send her dropping to her knees, gasping in surprise and pleasure. He felt his cock getting hard again even though it was the last thing he needed.

Jaimie let out a sudden gasp as her towel abruptly slipped loose of its own volition. Jake stared openly as it fell to the floor, his older sister now completely naked before him. She made to cover herself immediately but not before he'd gotten a generous glimpse of her pale, plump breasts, the faint blonde pubic hair adorning her perfect, mid-twenties pussy. She was fucking hot, but she was still his sister, and he would go to any length to win in their bickering.

"Jesus Christ, Jaimie!" he shouted. "Are you trying to make a point by flashing your flabby body at me?"

"Fuck you!" She hissed in frustration as she quickly knelt to grab her towel. "I am not flabby!"

"Get out of my room and go finish your shower!"

He made to push her backward, but she was already leaving. It was probably for the best that she didn't look back as she did. He had a shamefully obvious erection that would have been impossible to explain away if she'd seen it.

CHAPTER 6

Jake had no intention of staying in the house all day. He headed out almost immediately after his encounter with Jaimie, in no small part due to his lingering annoyance and frustration with her. He brought the remote with him.

He could have just as easily left it in his room, but there was a surreal aspect to its existence and how he'd found it. Part of him worried that it might simply disappear if he let it get too far away from him, ridiculous as the impulse was.

He considered how he might trace it back to whoever it belonged to. The simplest approach seemed to be just trying to turn it on, see if he heard anything vibrating from outside the door of his mother or sister's rooms while playing with the settings. He tried it as he was leaving. Nothing happened, which wasn't unexpected.

There were batteries within the thin device, but he was fairly certain they were dead. It took watch batteries, which was a little annoying, as he was sure he wouldn't be able to find any around the house. It gave him a clear enough objective for the day, however. He'd walk to the mall and look around to see what he could find in the department and electronics stores.

He remembered distantly that he didn't have to walk everywhere if he didn't want to. He'd bought a motorcycle in his senior year of high school, partially against the wishes of his fretting mother. Jake had left it in storage at a friend of his dad's, in a small shed on his property that he still had the key to. He'd even kept his motorcycle endorsement up to date.

It would be on the way to the mall, regardless, so he figured he'd swing by and see if the bike still started. And if it didn't, he might even be able to grab some of what he needed for the repairs in the same trip. He threw on some jeans and a light windbreaker and left the house.

Pinecross was mostly unchanged from the quiet little backwoods town he'd spent most of his young life in. It was familiar in a surreal way, with each change he encountered making him question his recollection. Hadn't there been a car dealership on the corner of Farell Street? Was that burger joint with a new name under new management?

He headed for the mall first since it would be on the way to his bike. He could have taken the bus, in theory, but walking felt helpful in terms of clearing his mind. The sky was overcast in a cold way, rather than one that promised rain, and he was glad he'd brought his windbreaker.

The way he usually took to the mall led him around the back side of it from his house. It was that fact that kept him from noticing right away that there were no cars in the sprawling parking lot out front, nor pedestrians milling around on the sidewalk. The mall was closed and had been for some time.

"Okay," he muttered. "Note to self. Not everything is exactly as it was before I'd left."

In a way, it almost seemed to reflect his dilemma with the remote and the mysterious sex toy, the changes he saw in Kate and Jaimie and even his mother. He was the one who'd left, the one lacking the context of the past four years.

The mall set him in an uneasy state of mind as he continued on to seek out his motorcycle. It was a long walk, almost forty minutes, the last portion of it down a sketchy, beaten up road with every other house abandoned. He was sure that it would be a similar situation, his bike lost to the elements or perhaps just missing entirely.

He was pleasantly surprised to find it right where he'd left it once he'd unlocked the shed, even covered with a blue tarp that his father's friend must have thrown on for extra security. He unwrapped it like a christmas gift, running his hand over the bars and feeling a flood of dumb memories rushing back to him. Racing around town like the teenage hoodlum he'd once been. Scenic rides along curvy hills. The horror of getting caught in the rain.

But would it start? That was the real question. He took it off the kick stand and wheeled it outside. It only sputtered on the first try, but that wasn't unusual. The wonderful purr it gave him on the second put a grin on his face. He pulled on his helmet, which he'd had the foresight to leave in the cargo net on the back and set off.

The ride home was exhilarating. He'd forgotten how free it made him feel, the wind roaring past, the sense of control as he navigated Pinecross's roads and streets. It was even more surreal at speed, racing down roads that he knew like the back of his hand while noticing all the little changes from time's inexorable forward flow.

He took a meandering route back to the house, arriving just before three. He parked the bike in the garage and took off his helmet. Making his way into the living room, he noticed that the cover for the hot tub in the backyard next to the pool was off. Jaimie must have been using it earlier, but that'd always been one of their mom's pet peeves.

He went outside onto the deck to cover it, less annoyed than he would have expected to be given he was cleaning up her mess. Jake only then remembered his clothes in the washer and hurried into the laundry room. He found them sitting atop the dryer, rather than within it, tossed aside by Jaimie who hadn't bothered to do him a similar favor.

His annoyance reached max capacity as he threw them in the dryer and started them up. He marched up to Jaimie's room and knocked on the door. Her music was blaring even louder than it had been last night.

"Put my clothes in the dryer next time!" he shouted. "And turn your music down!"

He didn't expect a response and he didn't get one. Jake took a deep breath and let it out, deciding that he was done bickering with his older sister for the day.

CHAPTER 7

Jake made himself a sandwich and got comfortable on the couch, watching TV for most of the rest of the afternoon. His mother and Kate arrived home around four. He greeted them with a wave as he brought his plate back into the kitchen.

"Mom," he said, smiling. "How was your day?"

"Long." She smiled and gave him a hug. "It's good to be home."

Jake was still adjusting to the hugs and the closeness. His mother's perfume would have stolen his attention had it not already been captured by the feeling of her soft, well-proportioned body against his. He breathed out as he stepped away from her, turning his focus to Kate.

"Hey Katie," he said. "How was school?"

She shrugged and didn't volunteer a real answer. Jake nodded and resisted the urge to pry. His mother was watching him, her gaze seeming almost analytical for a moment.

"Do you mind helping Kate with her homework?" she asked.

"Of course not," he said. "Assuming she wants me to."

"She does." His mother kicked off her heels and arched her back into a stretch that did interesting things to the pull of her breasts against her blouse. "She mentioned it on the drive home. I think she just felt too shy to ask you."

"She was never all that shy back before I left," muttered Jake. "Maybe a little shy, but never to this degree."

"She's... had a tough time at school."

Jake nodded. He headed upstairs, pausing outside Kate's room before knocking on the half open door.

"Katie?" he said. "Mind if I come in?"

"Sure."

He pushed the door open and found her sitting on her bed, her school uniform still on, along with a pair of socks patterned after the penguin character from the movie Mr. Popper's.

"Mom said you might need some help with your homework," he said.

She shrugged again. "Not really. Just need to get my computer working."

"What's wrong with it?"

"It won't go online." She walked over to her desk and shook the mouse to bring the monitor out of sleep. She opened the web browser and let out an annoyed sigh. "See?"

"Yup, that's definitely an offline computer," he said. "I can try a few things."

Kate let out an impossibly cute grumbling noise and clicked on a few bookmarks, which of course, didn't open. "I've tried everything already."

"Let me take a look."

He tried to sidle her out of the way, but she wouldn't move. He ended up stepping close behind her, sneaking his own hand onto the mouse. Kate stayed where she was, even pushing back for a surprising instant that put her petite butt in direct contact with Jake's crotch. He inhaled, catching a whiff of her girlish, teenage scent, red hair filling his field of view for a moment.

"Kate," he said, voice soft against the sudden quiet tension.

"Go ahead," she said. "Do whatever you'd normally do."

Jake shook his head and took control of the mouse. Kate didn't budge, staying in her position, pressed back against him. He could feel the curve of her butt as she brushed against him again, the subtle, girlish shape of her hips and her waist, and it was suddenly the hardest thing in the world to focus on anything but her petite body.

"How about this?" He tried disabling her internet connection.

"Maybe," said Katie.

He waited a few seconds. The strange tension reached a new peak. The idea that the remote might belong to Kate, his sweet little sister experimenting with kinky sex toys in secret, suddenly popped into his head. The scene of her moaning in bed seemed to flutter through his mind in vivid detail. He shifted forward as he enabled her connection again, his semi-hard cock briefly grinding into her ass in a manner that she must have felt.

"That's it," said Kate.

"Yeah?"

"Yeah." Her butt brushed one last time against his crotch as she cleared her throat and shifted to turn to face him. "It's back online. Thanks Jake."

She flashed a smile so innocent that it almost seemed cruel and patted him on the chest.

"Yeah..." he said. "No prob."

He turned to leave, glancing back at Kate as she sat down at her desk and resumed working. Jake made it back to his room and sat down on his bed. His erection was almost painful. The remote was burning a hole in his pocket, the temptation of learning which of them it belonged to suddenly seeming like the only thing that mattered in his life.

CHAPTER 8

Jake spent the next hour in his room, attempting to divine exactly what size and type of battery he needed for the remote. It was a far more obtuse task than he'd initially assumed it would be, with the different sizes of extremely similar watch batteries leading to a confusing situation that made him wish he could have simply found a battery that matched the dead ones in person earlier that day.

He got hungry as the evening arrived and went to see if his mother had already started cooking. She was in her office downstairs, but the door was open a crack. He paused before knocking, hearing her voice.

"That sounds challenging, Deborah," said Rebecca. "Have you tried incorporating toys into your relationship with Ted?"

Jake felt his heart skip a beat. Rebecca was having an online session with one of her patients. Eavesdropping was probably a huge ethical and privacy violation, but he was sure he'd just heard his mother mention sex toys.

"I'm not even sure how that conversation would go," said a woman's voice over the video call. "He would take it the wrong way if I suggested it. He'd think that he wasn't enough for me."

"I understand," said Rebecca. "It's important to consider his feelings in a situation like this. But I think it would be worth bringing up, especially if you communicate in a loving way, and tell him that it's not about him, but about your pleasure and your satisfaction. Your feelings matter too."

He crept even closer to the door. He would have placed his mother at the bottom of the list of suspected owners of the remote, but hearing what she was saying made it hard not to reconsider that assumption.

All he needed was for Deborah to ask the obvious question — did she ever use toys, herself? He felt his cock stirring in a confusing way as he considered how she might answer. Why did he want to hear that answer so badly? She was his mother, for god's sake.

"I'll think about it," said Deborah. "Thanks Rebecca. Same time next week?"

"Same time next week," said his mother.

Jake swore internally and took a few creeping steps away from the door.

"What the fuck were you just doing?" snapped Jaimie.

Jake whirled around, spotting his older sister at the bottom of the stairs. She was wearing a pink t-shirt with an upside down heart on the front that only stretched halfway down to cover her navel and baggy grey sweatpants.

"I was just going to ask Mom what we were having for dinner," he said, mostly truthfully. "What were you doing earlier when you took my clothes out of the washer and just left them on top of the dryer?"

"You just left them in there," said Jaimie, walking close by him on her way to the couch. "You expect me to do your load for you? I'm not touching your nasty boxers."

"They were clean. They'd just come out of the washer. God, you're unbelievable. I suppose I'll return the favor the next time your stuff gets in my way."

"Don't you dare put a hand on my stuff," she said, defiantly. "If I ever catch you touching my panties I'm going straight to Mom."

"Straight to mom about what?" asked Rebecca, as she came into the living room.

"Nothing," said Jaimie.

"Jaimie's just being annoying," said Jake.

"Fuck you, Jakey-kun."

"Hey." Rebecca wagged a finger at Jaimie. "Language. Can't the two of you at least try to get along?"

Jaimie rolled her eyes. Jake was just glad that she didn't follow up on her earlier question. He didn't particularly want his mother to know that he'd been eavesdropping, even if it was mostly by accident.

"Mom," he said. "What's for dinner?"

"I'm about to start it," she said. "How about pasta alfredo? It'll be quick."

"Sounds good to me," said Jake.

"Didn't we just have that a couple days ago?" groaned Jaimie.

"Is there anything you don't complain about?" asked Jake.

Jaimie glowered at him. Rebecca sighed and headed into the kitchen. Jake watched her go, catching sight of her skirt as she turned a corner, how it hugged her hips and butt. The image of his mother and one of her patients talking about sex toys was still in his head, and he felt uncomfortable at how hot and bothered it got him.

"I'm going to play a game," said Jaimie.

She flopped down onto the couch and grabbed the controller for their family's Nintendo Switch. Jake was still slightly annoyed with her, but saw the chance to perhaps smooth down some of the friction.

"Push over," he said. "And pass me the second controller."

Jaimie furrowed her brow, but a tiny smile crept onto her face. "Fine, Jakey-kun. Just don't get mad about losing to a girl when I demolish you."

Jake chuckled and turned his controller on as she passed it to him. Jaimie launched Super Smash Bros from the home screen, one of their old favorites from back when they'd still been close growing up. Jake felt a warm sense of nostalgia, or maybe just the urge to tease her.

"I still remember the Christmas when we first got the version of this on the Wii," said Jaimie. "Remember how mad you got the first time I beat you at this?"

"No, but I remember the last time, when you almost broke the controller." Jake brushed his shoulders off as she brought up the character select screen. "Hopefully you cherish that memory. Plenty of people were all about Smash at my college and I've gotten way better. You'll never beat me again."

"I bet that's just about all the smashing you were doing," said Jaimie, mockingly.

The jibe struck a little too close to home as Jake thought of Estelle, her parting words after torpedoing their relationship. His face felt hot, but he kept smiling through the anger, annoyed at Jaimie while knowing it was unfair to dump on her.

"Pick your character," he said.

"Done." She picked Hyrule Temple as their level, which was one of the few they'd always agreed upon. The timer counted down, and the fight began.

Jake held his own, but only at the start. It was true that he had played a fair amount of Super Smash Bros. while away at college, but it hadn't exactly been his focus. He hadn't been the best player at his school either, not by a long shot. Jaimie was simply on a different level in a way that left him wondering if she'd been training for this exact moment.

"Give up yet?" she asked, taunting him as she spiked him off the level.

"Nope."

Jake concentrated, trying his best to dodge and block and counter her attacks as he respawned. Jaimie was laughing at him, which only added to his seething annoyance as his defeat slowly became inevitable.

"How about now?" she asked, knocking him out a second time.

"I don't think you understand, Jaimie." He reached over and started mushing buttons on her controller. "I'll go to any length to win."

"You ass!" she said, laughing.

She grabbed at his controller and the action of their characters suddenly seemed to mirror their movements on the couch. They tugged and grappled for each other's controllers. Jake had a much more pronounced strength advantage outside of the game.

He yanked on Jaimie's controller, pulling both it and her backward. She still refused to let go, to the point where she fell forward onto him as he tipped sideways on the couch. He felt a confused, flustered rush of emotions as Jaimie's body collided against his. She was soft, but the way her breasts and thighs pressed into him was vaguely sexual and dangerous.

"Give it to me," she muttered, still grabbing at both their controllers.

"I don't think so," he said.

Jake wrapped his arms around her waist, pinning her controller against her stomach. Jaimie wriggled against him, her body seeming to grind and press into his in a way that made his heart race.

She had big tits and a really nice ass. He absently thought about how quickly he'd be getting turned on if it was someone outside his family who looked similar, or even if it was just her with a mask on or a bag over her head. Acknowledging it made it real in that same perverse way, and he felt himself getting hard at a sprint.

"Jake!" shouted Jaimie.

He tried to quickly yank the controller from her hand, knowing she'd never let him live it down if she noticed he was getting an erection. Jaimie struggled and writhed against him, and Jake felt her butt rub directly into his crotch. She let out a surprised and sexy gasp and immediately froze.

"Jaimie!" shouted Rebecca, from the kitchen. "Jake! Kate! Dinner's ready."

"You hear that, Jake?" Jaimie was still against him, and he swore he felt her hips flex slightly. "Dinner's ready."

"Jaimie..." he muttered, finally letting go of the controller. "Get off me."

"You're too easy, Jakey-kun."

She made another unbelievably hot noise as she leaned backward, putting her butt in thighs in undeniable contact with his hardening cock as she climbed off him. Jake watched her walk into the kitchen, hips swaying in fascinating ways underneath the grey fabric of her sweatpants.

CHAPTER 9

Dinner was a quiet affair. Jake picked up on a similar tension to what he'd felt that morning and suspected that family meals hadn't been a regular thing before his arrival back. Kate ate quietly, Jaimie had her phone out, and his mother seemed to be distracted.

"This is good, Mom," he said.

"Hmm?" Rebecca blinked a few times, as if coming out of a daydream. "Oh. Thank you, Jake. I can make it more often if you'd like?"

"Who cares what he'd like?" muttered Jaimie.

Jake kicked one of her legs under the table. Jaimie kicked him back. Rebecca sighed, and Kate stared down at her plate.

"Kate," said Rebecca. "Did you talk with Jake about your homework?"

"A little," said Kate.

"She said she needed help with her computer," he said. "It was offline earlier, but I fixed it for her."

"That was nice of Jake," said Rebecca.

Kate nodded, and not much else was said during the meal. He helped his mother clear the table and insisted on loading the dishwasher.

"It is beyond good to have you home, Jake." Rebecca touched his shoulder as he was moving plates onto the rack. "I love you."

"I love you too, Mom," he said. "It's good to be home."

She hugged him from behind and kissed his cheek. A hot shudder ran through him and his mind jumped back to wrestling on the couch with Jaimie, and even before that, pressed up against Kate as he'd worked on her computer. The common element in all of those awkwardly hot situations was clearly him.

He needed to get laid. Badly. Moreover, he needed to find a girlfriend who would give him some practice so he could move beyond his own issues and insecurities. It seemed like such a stupid problem to have, especially if it was compounding to complicate his relationships with his family.

There wasn't much else to do but head upstairs after he was done starting the dishwasher. He wished everyone else a good night and headed to bed.

***

"Still up?"

Jake came down the stairs slowly, deep into the night. He saw Jaimie sitting on the couch in a baggy t-shirt, illuminated only by the TV. She had a game controller back in her hand and was playing Super Smash Bros. again.

"Yeah," she whispered. "I couldn't sleep. Want to go another round?"

"I don't know." He stifled a yawn, but took a step closer to the couch. "It's pretty late."

"I'll make it more interesting." Jaimie shifted sideways, making room for him with a teasing smile. "Winner gets to make the loser do whatever they want."

"What?"

"You heard me."

He couldn't resist. "Anything I want?"

"Sure. But you won't beat me, so it hardly matters."

He returned her smile and picked up a controller, already feeling himself getting weirdly excited. Jaimie had made him an intriguing offer, but she was also his sister, and the game and her deal seemed like an obvious trap. One which he unfortunately couldn't resist. Jake felt his heart beating a little faster as the timer counted down and the fight began.

Jaimie was good, but not as good as she'd been earlier that night. Jake wondered if perhaps she was tired, or maybe he had extra motivation now that the stakes had been raised. Jaimie clearly seemed frustrated as he pulled ahead with the first kill.

"Not bad." She shifted sideways on the couch and let her feet settle into his lap. "But it's not over yet."

Jake blinked, suddenly finding it hard to concentrate. Jaimie had her socks off, which seemed weird to him given how cold it was. She wiggled her toes, brushing them directly over his cock.

"Hey," he said, as she picked up an invincibility star. "No fair."

"Anything goes, Jakey-kun."

Her foot started to move. Jake groaned as he felt himself getting hard, but never lost focus. Jaimie began to make little noises as he beat her down, sexy and pouty sighs and grumbles. Her foot never stopped moving, big toe running up the length of his cock as he reached full hardness. There was no way she didn't feel it.

But in the end, he won. He looked at Jaimie, smiling but uncertain, as the post fight stats came up.

"I won," he said.

"I guess. Whatever."

"So now you have to do what I want," he said. The tension in the room was palpable.

"Yup." Jaimie slid closer to him on the couch. "But I think I already know what you want."

He couldn't believe it... but he could. His sister was a total freak, a shameless slut, a fact he'd only missed because of how her bitchiness had obscured it. He reached out a hand and touched her cheek, thumb running just under her bottom lip. He started to guide her face down toward his crotch, and she let out another sexy pouting noise, and then...

***

Jake's alarm on his phone went off. He groaned and slapped a hand toward it, annoyed beyond belief. For once, he could remember every detail of the dream he'd been woken up from. Which was unfortunate, given how fucked up it had been.

He tried to banish it from his mind, but that only seemed to conjure the specifics deeper into focus. He wished he could at least get rid of his morning wood, but the idea of trying to get off to porn or his own imagination seemed like it would give the dream even more illicit power.

He settled for slow breathing as he put together an outfit for the day. Most of his clothing was still downstairs in the laundry room, and he settled for track pants and a ratty but serviceable sweatshirt. He stopped to consider the remote once more as he found it on his desk.

The fact that finding batteries for it was still at the top of his priority list made him stop and wonder about just how aimless his life had become. He thought about his absentee father, completely removed from the family situation. He was on the opposite end of the spectrum, home and harboring a growing obsession.

He stuffed the remote into his pocket and went downstairs. Jaimie was in the kitchen, thankfully dressed in actual clothing, with her phone out as she stared at the countertop.

"Morning Jake," she said.

"Morning Jaimie," he said, looking for the coffee. "Plans for today?"

"None of your business," she said, though her voice was gentle.

Rebecca and Kate arrived not long after. Rebecca was in a business skirt and blouse and Kate was back in her school uniform. Jake found himself staring at his younger sister, his mind jumping back to the dream he'd woken up from. Kate blushed, perhaps noticing his attention.

"Good morning Jake," said Rebecca. "Good morning Jaimie."

Jaimie grunted, still focused on her phone. Kate sat down at the table and started eating a bowl of cereal. Jake found himself watching her again, noticing the way her lips pursed as she ate, and the delicate, demure movements of her hand as she brushed a few loose strands of red hair out of her face.

"Jake?" asked Rebecca. "I noticed you got your bike out of storage."

"Yeah," he said. "Thought I might need a better way of getting around town than just walking."

"Think you could pick Kate up from school today? I have an appointment that might run past three."

"Yeah, no prob." He smiled at Kate, amused by how she simultaneously smiled back and glanced away. "She can't just take the bus? Not that I mind, just curious."

Kate shrugged. "I don't like the bus."

"Fair enough. I could use an excuse to roll around town on my bike anyway."

"Do you mind parking in the church lot?" asked Kate, in a quiet voice. "The one across from the school."

"Yeah, sure."

Jake accepted some coffee as his mother finally finished brewing it and brought him a mug. He took a sip and let himself relax.

CHAPTER 10

Kate and Rebecca left a few minutes later. Jaimie meandered back up to her room. Jake spent most of his morning working out in the basement gym, which had actually been expanded in his time away. His dad had kept a pool table on one side of the basement, but it had either been given away or sold, replaced by a matted area that his mother presumably used for her yoga.

The gym equipment was top notch, including a bench press with a weight stack. Jake did some squats, some dead lifts, and a few sets with the weights, taking it easy since his body still felt somewhat fatigued. He called it quits around noon and took a shower. Jaimie was in the kitchen when he came down.

"Hey Jakey-kun," she said. "I'm craving ice cream and we're out."

"Do I look like your Doordash driver?"

"Don't be a dick. I'll give you money for it. Please?" She leaned forward, pouting in a way that reminded Jake altogether way too much of his dream.

He let out a sigh. "What flavor?"

"Cookie dough. Thanks little bro."

She gave him the money and he headed out. It was a gorgeous fall day, the air crisp and cool and the sky a brilliant blue. Jake took his bike out of the garage, revving the engine as he cruised through Pinecross.

He decided to head downtown, through an area with some miscellaneous shops. It was an eclectic mixture of businesses, ranging from a tattoo parlor and an antique store to a pawn shop and a local clothing boutique. There was a small electronics store, Ryan's Retro Repair, one of the dying variety that offered repairs for just about anything.

He made his way in and was greeted to the sight of a tanned young man watching a subtitled anime movie or series on a monitor while opening up an original grey GameBoy. Jake glanced around for batteries as he made his way over to the counter.

"Hey," he said. "Are you Ryan."

"No. Lorenzo."

"Shouldn't it be Lorenzo's Repair or something, then?" joked Jake.

"You should take that up with the owner, who I am not," said Lorenzo. "What can I help you with?"

"Do you sell those watch batteries here?" he asked.

"What type?" asked Lorenzo. "Or if you have your watch with you just pass it this way."

Jake only briefly thought about showing him the remote before stopping to consider basic discretion. The last thing he wanted was to have to explain anything surrounding the context, and lying felt like too much effort.

"About yay big," he said, pinching his fingers together. "Tiny little discs."

Lorenzo nodded and pulled open a drawer behind the counter. Jake stared in awe at one of the most impressive messes he'd ever seen in a two by three-foot space. Lorenzo shot his hand downward, rifled around for a few seconds, and pulled out a pack of four watch batteries encased in plastic packaging. Brand new.

"Here." He tossed them onto the counter. "Take them."

"How much?"

"Just take them," said Lorenzo. "They're like three bucks a pack and we don't sell them here anyway. Those are just some I had laying around I don't need."

Jake raised his eyebrows. "Cool. Thanks, man. You sure?"

"Yeah, don't worry about it," he said. "Just remember Ryan's if you need something repaired."

"Still think it should be called Lorenzo's," he said.

He hung out for a few minutes and they chatted about anime. Jake had watched all the popular stuff when he'd been younger, earning him his nickname from Jaimie. Lorenzo had good taste, for the most part.

"Take it easy, Lorenzo," he said, finally leaving.

"You too."

He still had time before picking up Kate, so he went to the park and sat in the sun. The idea of going on a longer ride appealed to him, but his bank account was running on fumes and his bike would be too if he zipped around carelessly. He suspected that his next move, assuming he stayed in the area, would be to look for a job.

He ended up getting to Kate's school a little early and parked his bike in the church lot. It was a different school than he'd gone to - his father had insisted on a boys' only boarding school that he'd hated rather than a normal public school. He pulled his helmet off and leaned back, enjoying the weather. Students started filing out a few minutes after three.

Jake was about to head off and look for her when heavy footsteps accompanied by someone clearing their throat intervened to harsh his mellow.

"You can't park your bike there," said a man, with a rough smoker's voice.

Jake climbed off his bike, turning to look at a tall priest, black clothed and white collar. He was completely bald and had an odd scar across his otherwise shiny head.

"I'm just picking someone up from the school," he said. "I'll be gone in five minutes, I promise."

He caught sight of Kate leaving school. She came out the side door, rather than the front, where most of the students were pouring out in search of their cars or busses or after school activities. He still wondered why she wasn't involved in some club or team, something to occupy her and keep her involved socially.

"This is a private lot!" barked the priest. "No heathen motorcycles! Get!"

"Relax," said Jake. "I'm already on my way..."

He trailed off as he noticed that Kate wasn't alone. A group of similarly aged and uniformed teenagers were following her, mostly girls, but with at least one boy who was walking backwards just in front of her. Jake felt an odd flash of brotherly jealousy for a second, but the situation quickly revealed itself as something else.

One of the girls behind Kate snuck forward to strip her backpack's shoulder straps most of the way down. The boy grabbed the bag and quickly tossed it to one of the other girls. Kate came to a stop, looking at her bag with a defeated expression for a few seconds before dropping her gaze to her feet.

Jake felt a cold, creeping rage come over him.

"I'll call a tow truck!" snapped the priest. "Stupid kids always trying to park here instead of at the school like they should! Don't test me, I will have you towed! I assure you I will!"

One of the girls unzipped Kate's bag and poured the contents onto the sidewalk. Jake's rage flared hot.

"Touch my fucking bike and I just might do something worthy of confession, Father," he said, whirling to get into the priest's face. "I'm picking up my sister and then leaving. Deal with it."

The priest seethed, his entire face turning a shade of pinkish red, veins bulging through his forehead. "God have mercy on your soul!"

Jake turned back and saw Kate picking up her stuff, the gaggle of bullies having departed. Other students were still hurrying by on their way to wherever they were going, however, kicking her lunchbox, stepping on her notebooks.

He knew what Kate had asked, but he couldn't stop himself from climbing back onto his bike and riding directly to her. He parked in the school's pickup lane and turned his bike off.

"Hey."

He expected her to chastise him for not listening to her, but she didn't. She looked up at him, clearly trying to keep her composure, and burst into tears. Jake grabbed the rest of her stuff and pulled her into a tight hug.

"Let's get you home," he whispered.

CHAPTER 11

To his credit, Jake did manage to remember that Jaimie had wanted her ice cream. He stopped at a gas station on the way home, heart still aching for Kate after seeing what she'd been through.

"Do you want anything?" he asked.

She shook her head, the motion slightly comical with a motorcycle helmet on. Her eyes were still red and she still hadn't spoken.

He found the ice cream freezer. He literally didn't have enough money for more than one carton, so he opted for cherry chunk, Kate's favorite flavor, suspecting that Jaimie wouldn't care that much. He held it out to his little sister as they climbed back onto the bike.

"Put this in your bag for me?" he asked.

She nodded, but didn't smile. He felt her wrap her arms around him as he started his bike up and they rode the last of the distance home. He parked it in the garage and took her helmet.

"Kate..." he said. "I'm sorry."

She shrugged. Jake had a sudden impulse. He pulled her into a tight hug and just kept her in his arms for long enough to let her know how much he cared. He kissed her on the top of her head and tried to look into her eyes. She glanced away.

"Talk to me," he said. "What's going on? How can I help?"

She shook her head and picked her bag up, stopping only to take the ice cream out and offer it to him on the way to the house. Jake sighed and brought it into the kitchen. Jaimie was playing video games in the living room.

"You should have ice cream and change for me," she said, not looking away from the TV.

"Change is a whopping seventeen cents," said Jake. "Ice cream is in the freezer."

Jaimie immediately got up, intent on satisfying her craving. Jake sighed and started to make his way up to his room.

"Hey!" cried Jaimie. "I asked for cookie dough!"

He came back down, but not for the argument that Jaimie's fuming expression demanded.

"How long has Kate been getting bullied at school?" he asked.

"Oh..." said Jaimie. "She doesn't really eat ice cream anymore, for future reference."

"This isn't a recent development, is it?"

Jaimie shook her head. "I thought it had died down recently. She really struggled with it as a freshman and sophomore. Mom was calling the school almost every week trying to figure out what could be done. They never gave a shit."

Jake let out a frustrated breath, feeling the cold rage again. Jaimie put her hands on her hips.

"She didn't want you to know," said Jaimie. "I think she's reached the point where she's internalized the shame."

"That's fucked up."

"I agree," said Jaimie. She opened the cherry chunk ice cream and began scooping some into a bowl. "I worry about her a lot, you know. If you come up with anything you think might help, I'm all ears."

Jake nodded slowly. He started to turn back toward the stairs.

"Hey," she said. "Bring this to her."

"I thought you said she doesn't really eat ice cream anymore?"

"Still worth trying. I mean, it is ice cream."

Jake snorted and took the bowl. He went up to Kate's room, pausing to listen for a second or two and hearing nothing.

"Katie?" he said. "I brought you some ice cream."

No response. He knocked again, and then decided to try the door. It was unlocked. Kate was stretched out on her bed, watching something on her phone. He saw her pause it as he stepped inside and set the bowl down on her bedside table.

"Cherry chunk," he said. "Your favorite, right?"

"Sometimes," she said, quietly.

Jake knew better than to try to force her to open up to him, especially about something as painful as being bullied. Still, he had so many questions. It made him feel like he was failing in his capacity as her brother to not be able to help her, swoop in and problem solve, and if needed, crack some heads.

"Kate..." he said. "Is there anything I can do?"

"No," she said. "I don't think so."

"I just..." Jake felt frustration building in his chest, hot and heavy. "I want you to know that you can come to me, okay?"

"I know." She took a bite of the ice cream and gave him a heartbreaking smile. "It isn't so bad. Just for one more year."

He nodded, but wasn't sure he agreed, based off what little he'd seen. It was likely that the bullying was happening in school, as well, not just in the short glimpse he'd gotten of her leaving at the end of the day.

"It started when I was a freshman," she said. "Remember how the middle schools all merge into Pinecross High?"

"I remember," he said.

Even though he'd gone to a different school, he'd seen Jaimie go through it when she'd first reached ninth grade.

"I didn't know all that many people given how small my middle school was," muttered Kate. "I was just alone, trying to meet people but never knowing what to say. Even that wasn't so bad, though. It was lonely, but there are worse things than being alone, you know? I like being alone a lot of the time. It was also back when I still had my braces. Remember how nerdy and stupid I used to look?"

The words came in a jumbled flood, the most Jake could recently remember her speaking at once. She stopped at the end and glanced away.

"You looked cute, not nerdy or stupid," he said. He put an arm around her shoulders.

"If you say so," she muttered.

He waited for her to continue, but somewhat expectantly, she didn't.

"Keep going," he said. "I want to hear it all."

"It's boring and stupid," she muttered. "You don't care."

"I do care," he said. "And if you don't keep going I'm going to steal your ice cream."

He made to reach over her and grab the bowl. She swatted his hand, a smile briefly stealing onto her face.

"I made an instagram account because everybody else was," she muttered. "But nobody followed me. Well, some people did, but barely anybody. None of the cool kids. Until..." She shrugged and glanced away from him. "This guy Daniel followed me. From another school. With lots of friends and cool photos and he was a skateboarder. And he started liking everything I posted, and he'd message and say hey or ask me how I was doing. And then he asked me if I would be his... girlfriend."

Jake felt another stab of brotherly jealousy, but suppressed it with his concern. He still had an arm around her and rubbed her shoulder and upper arm with his hand.

"I'm listening. What happened?"

"Nothing." She shook her head. "I never met him in person. He always had a reason why he couldn't. He said he lived far away and had to get a long ride to school. Then when it was vacation and I asked Mom if she'd drive me he said he was away. But I didn't care. It wasn't a big deal. He made me feel like I mattered, you know, and..."

Jake pulled her closer to him, suspecting he knew where it was headed.

"He wanted pictures of me." Her voice was a whisper, but her eyes went suddenly serious. "And videos. I never sent him nudes! There were some in my underwear, but never anything more. I'm not a complete idiot. He also asked me to... do things. Sent me a couple of gifts, but that was all near the end, and..."

She looked so wounded. Jake wished he could go back in time and protect her.

"It was all made up," she whispered. "When Daniel finally said he was coming to my school to meet me and asked me to wait for him, I waited. He never showed up, but Beth and Shayla and Dean and the rest of the assholes did. They had a fullsize printout of 'Daniel' and they taunted me and asked if I still wanted to kiss him all over like I'd said in my messages. I pushed Beth and knocked her into the mud and... that was when the real bullying began, I guess. After that."

Jake pulled Kate into a hug. She was stiff and resistant, but started to relax as he gently stroked her hair and back.

"Katie," he whispered. "You didn't do anything wrong. Those kids were evil. I can't imagine how much that must have hurt."

"I'm over it."

He heard her sniffle and could feel wet tears against his shirt where her face was pressed.

"Do you want to watch a movie tonight?" he suggested. "Your choice. We can hang out on the couch. I'll make some popcorn, even."

"I don't know," she muttered. "Maybe after."

She shifted out of his embrace and lay down on her bed. Jake stayed with her for a few minutes before getting up and heading to the door.

"I love you, Katie."

"I love you Jake. I'm glad you're back."

CHAPTER 12

Rebecca was just getting home as Jake came downstairs. She had two pizza boxes in hand which she set down on the counter with a tired sigh.

"I hope you don't mind pizza for dinner, Jake," she said. "I am exhausted."

"Pizza is perfect," he said. "Kate and I were going to hang out on the couch and watch a movie."

Rebecca kicked off her heels and glanced back at him. "You manage to pick her up alright this afternoon?"

"I suppose you could say that."

Rebecca gave him a pained smile. She leaned forward against the kitchen island, the posture doing interesting things with her breasts and cleavage within the professional white blouse she had on.

"I wish she'd just tell me more about what's going on with her," said Rebecca. "Kate is so reserved and quiet. Jaimie is the opposite."

"She's a tough nut to crack," said Jake. "She's being bullied."

Rebecca sighed. "I hoped it had stopped, but knowing her, she's just been stoically and quietly enduring it."

"Have you talked to the school?"

"Numerous times, along with the parents of some of the kids who I know are a part of it," said Rebecca. "Kate won't tell me anything specific anymore. Jaimie was even trying to help at one point, talking to siblings from her time at Pinecross High."

Jake had more questions, but Kate came downstairs before he could get any of them off. He thought about what she'd told him, and his mind reluctantly made the connection between the remote and vibrator and the supposed gifts that Daniel had sent.

Kate had said that there were no nudes in the possession of her tormentor, but that phrasing still left a lot of wiggle room. Had she gotten a Master Pulse as a gift? Had she used it, filmed herself clothed, but sexually engaged?

He was a bastard of a brother for letting the thought turn him on. Kate was smiling, even though her eyes were faintly red around the edges. She walked over and kissed him on the cheek.

"Hey Mom," she said. "Pizza for dinner? Did you get the broccoli one?"

"Yes, I got the broccoli one," said Rebecca, smiling. "You should offer some to Jake."

"Do I want to try this?" he asked, smiling.

"Trust me," said Kate. "You'll like it."

It was a surprisingly happy and hopeful mood, despite Kate's rough afternoon of bullying and revelations. Jaimie even came down for a minute, hovering around the periphery with a slice of pepperoni pizza while everyone else talked about their day.

"Isn't it bad luck to argue with priests?" asked Jaimie, after he'd given them an abridged version of the drama he'd went through parking his bike.

"That's a superstition," said Jake.

"How about we focus on positive solutions next time?" suggested Rebecca. "Sweetie, you could have just moved your bike."

"People park in that lot all the time," said Jake. "At least they used to."

Kate had slipped upstairs for something. Jake went up after her, wanting to check in with her about watching a movie while the living room TV was still available. Her door was open a crack and he didn't think anything about pushing it the rest of the way open.

"How does pizza and The Princess Diaries... sound?"

He stared in surprise and no small amount of awe at Kate's nude chest. She'd been picking out pajamas, apparently. Her tits were on the small side, but only compared to Jaimie and his mother.

Solid b-cups, pale with pink and perky nipples. She had on her glasses, her panties, and nothing else beyond an expression of surprise matching his own. He felt an odd but compelling stirring within him and knew he'd never get the image out of his mind.

"Sorry!" He whipped around and hopped back out into the hallway, closing the door.

"It's okay," said Kate. "Um. I'll be right down."

Jake hurried downstairs. Rebecca was in the kitchen, looking at something on her phone. Jaimie was nowhere to be seen, presumably out for the night.

"Are you alright, Jake?" asked Rebecca. "Your face is flushed."

"I'm fine," he said, trying and failing to get Kate's naked tits out of his head.

"I think Jaimie mentioned something about a party tonight. I doubt she'll be back before midnight." Rebecca yawned. "Myself, I'm exhausted. Tomorrow is my day off and I plan on doing nothing more than loafing around the house."

"Sounds like fun," he said. He took a deep breath, trying to will down an unnecessary and evil erection.

His mother headed upstairs and a few minutes later, Kate came down. Looking at her with her firm breasts still so vividly in his mind was like looking at the sun, best done through quick glances and off angles. She had on a baggy T-shirt and boy shorts and pink fuzzy socks, red hair loose against her shoulders.

"I like The Princess Diaries," she said, after an awkward pause.

"I thought so," said Jake. "I'll put it on. Grab me a slice of pizza?"

"Sure."

He got the TV set up and took one side of the couch. Kate came back into the living room with pizza for them both along with drinks. She gave him a mischievous smile as she passed him his.

"Here," she said. "Let me know what you think."

He took a sip, tasting carbonation and something else. "Did you spike this?"

"It's Sprite mixed with some of Mom's wine," whispered Kate.

"Katie," he said, smiling despite some valid concerns. "You're eighteen. I doubt Mom would approve of you drinking. Even less so of you sneaking some secretly."

"She doesn't have to know everything," said Kate.

He let his gaze meet hers and again felt like he was looking at the sun. Her expression was so mischievous and playful, her pale skin and freckled cheeks rosy with excitement.

"I'm your older brother," he said. "I might have some justified reservations, but I won't snitch on you."

"I knew you wouldn't."

CHAPTER 13

Kate grabbed a blanket before taking a spot on the far end of the couch. It was a little chilly, and Jake motioned at the comforter with his hand.

"Mind sharing that with me?"

"Of course not," she said. "Do you mind if I stretch out?"

Jake shook his head and found himself with both the blanket and his little sister's feet in his lap. He touched them on reflex and then let go, unsure of what to do with his hands. Kate didn't seem to notice or care. She rubbed her fuzzy sock clad feet together like she was trying to warm them up, coming to a stop after shifting them around with one draped across his crotch.

He wondered if he should try to subtly shift them away, but after a second it seemed like it was too late to object. She wriggled her toes and he felt the movement along the edge of his cock, along with his body's innate, unstoppable reaction. It didn't matter that she was his little sister, innocent and vulnerable. It should have mattered.

"I love this movie," whispered Kate.

"Yeah," he said. "Same."

He managed to focus on the movie to an extent. Anne Hathaway was a great actor, and Kate's giggling was infectious. She never really stopped moving her feet. Jake eventually had a full-blown erection under the blanket and had to shift in creative ways to keep her toes from bumping into it directly.

But he could only do so much. Kate shifted at one point and her foot all but slid up the entire length of his hard cock. A dark part of him delighted at the contact and had been waiting for it, hoping for it. His sensible, older brother side was mortified, even more so as Kate suddenly pulled away and stood up.

"Need a refill?" She took his glass.

"Sure," he said, letting out the breath he'd been holding.

When she came back with two cups that looked distinctly more wine than sprite, she set them down on the coffee table. Instead of going back to her old spot, she slid right up against him, not unlike how she used to cuddle into his side when they were both much younger.

"Katie," he said, smiling, but not pushing her away.

"Jake." She blinked, still smiling, breath heavy with wine. "Am I really that much of a total loser?"

"You're not a loser, Katie." He put an arm around her and kissed her on the head. "You are somewhat drunk, however."

"Am I ugly, then? Is that why?"

She blinked a few times. It was hard to tell whether they were tipsy tears or something more. Jake ached for his little sister, either way.

"You are so far from ugly Katie that it's hilarious you'd even ask that," he muttered.

"Really?"

She blinked up at him, eyes wide and moist, and slid in even closer. One of her hands settled on his thigh. Jake shifted nervously, aware of how close her fingers were to what remained of his erection. That horrible dichotomy of desires snuck up on him again, intrigued by the contact while terrified by what would happen if she noticed his arousal.

"You're gorgeous, Katie. Gorgeous, cute, pretty, whatever word you want to call it. But you shouldn't feel like you need to be, you know? You should just be happy being you."

"I'm so happy you're my brother, Jake."

Kate leaned in even closer, definitely drunk. She stared at his mouth, eyes sinking down until they were half lidded. The dark voice was there again, pushing him forward. She still needed comfort and convincing, and who better to get it from than the one man in her life who would never betray her?

"Katie..." he whispered.

Her hand settled on his thigh, the tip of her index finger making definite contact with his erection. He could do more than just kiss her. They were both drunk, alone on the couch, watching a movie.

The front door suddenly swung open. Jake jerked away from Kate as though she'd just pulled a gun on him. Jaimie had music playing over her phone's speaker as she came into the living room, noisily kicking her shoes off.

"What was that?" asked Jaimie. "Why'd you freak out like that? Do you have a girl over, Jake?"

"No!" he snapped. "It's just me and Katie."

"Oh." Jaimie came closer and sucked in a breath. "Oh!"

Jake was mortified, but tried to play it cool like he was watching the movie. His heart beat faster and sank into his chest simultaneously. Jaimie's voice had that telltale edge to it. They'd been caught.

"You're drinking Mom's wine again, aren't you?" asked Jaimie.

"She never notices," muttered Kate.

"She will if you finish an entire bottle, you dork," said Jaimie. "Jake, aren't you supposed to be an older brother and veto your little sister's illegal behavior?"

"As though you ever did that with me, big sister," he said, relaxing a little.

Jaimie opened the freezer and groaned. "I still can't believe you didn't get me my cookie dough ice cream. You owe me for that."

"Jaimie wanted cookie dough?" asked Kate.

"Jaimie will eat any flavor of ice cream, whereas you have always been picky," he said, smiling.

"Thanks Jake," whispered Kate.

She leaned in and kissed him on the cheek, keeping her face close to his afterward. The smell of wine on her breath set off a horrible rise of heat and emotion within him.

They stayed at a more sensible distance from one another for the rest of the movie. Kate was asleep when it finished. Jake scooped her up and carried her to bed in the same way he used to when she was little, tucking her in and kissing her on the forehead before retiring to his own room.

CHAPTER 14

Jake was the first one downstairs the next morning and had the honor and privilege of cleaning and starting up the coffee maker. Kate had left the bottle of wine she'd been pilfering from out on the counter as well, and he recorked it and put it away in the wine cabinet, though it was obvious that it'd been tampered with.

He still couldn't get his memory of the previous night out of his head. Kate had been drunk, clearly, but the way she'd been looking at him and playing around under the blanket had unveiled a hidden desire within him. One which he knew he could never indulge in, the kind of desire that was better suited to being buried in a deep hole and never thought about, never acted upon.

It still galled him that she'd asked if she was ugly. The bullying truly had gotten deep into her psyche for her to harbor an insecurity like that for even a second. She was undeniably pretty, maybe not busty, maybe not classically beautiful like a super model, but the kind of girl who, outside of the pointless cliques of high school, could date whoever she wanted.

Jaimie came downstairs. Jake had almost become used to her scanty morning outfits, today a teal tank top and grey yoga pants, but being used to it was an issue in itself. His gaze lingered for longer than normal and Jaimie noticed, narrowing her eyes defiantly at him as she marched toward the coffee.

"Is it ready?" she asked, with a tired groan.

"About to be."

He set a hand on the pot to pour himself some. Jaimie tried to slide in front of him to pour hers first.

"Out of my way, Jakey-kun," she muttered.

His frustration flared and he pushed out with his hand, aiming for her shoulder, but grazing one of her breasts instead. Jaimie glared at him rather than freaking out and pushed back, moving herself more than him with the force of the movement.

"Move, Jakey-kun."

"Make me."

Jaimie smirked and stepped closer. Jake's gaze was instantly drawn to her chest, her tits bouncing slightly. Was every morning going to be like this? Every encounter with Jaimie as petulant and frustrating as when they'd been foolish children?

"Pour me some?" she asked.

She slid the mug she'd grabbed for herself closer in the same movement as she stepped in nearer to him, almost grinding into his side. Jake hesitated, caught off guard by the tone of the power play.

"Sure," he said. "See, all you had to do was ask nicely."

"I'll keep that in mind for future reference," said Jaimie.

She did a stretch that pushed her breasts and stomach forward, all but begging Jake to sneak a glance at them. He did, and he saw the way she noticed, how she smirked as though she'd won some kind of hidden prize. It was infuriating, but fair play.

"You should go check on Kate," said Jaimie. "I've seen her sneak wine before. She's a total lightweight."

Jake started pouring his own coffee, mind shifting gears toward his other sister. "Does she drink often?"

"I mean, not super often, but it is turning into a bit of a habit for her," said Jaimie.

"Do you think it's a reaction to her school situation?"

"The bullying?" Jaimie shrugged. "I honestly don't know. I guess I am a little worried about it, but ratting her out to Mom seems like the last thing that would help."

She let out a sigh and Jake felt as though he'd found at least one thing they agreed on. He poured a mug of coffee for Kate and went up to her room. He knocked and heard a muffled "come in" in a somewhat hungover sounding voice. Without thinking anything more of it, he swung the door open.

Jake blinked in surprise. Kate was laying in bed, in her underwear, one leg still under her sheet but otherwise completely exposed. She'd clearly just woken up, based off the sleepy look on her face and the way her hair was sprawled out in a red, tangled mess. Her bra was black and lacy, her panties light pink and cotton.

"Hey Jake," she mumbled. "Morning."

"Uh, morning Katie." He set the mug of coffee down on her bedside table and tried not to stare. "How are you feeling?"

"Like I got hit by a truck," she muttered. "And then run over by a cement mixer."

"Ouch. Coffee might help."

She reached out a hand and made a grabbing motion. He started to move the mug into her fingers but she grabbed at him, instead. He let her pull him onto her bed where she hugged him from the side as he sat next to her. It was so girlish and little sisterly, but also problematic given her undressed state. Jake patted her head and slowly began to stand up.

"Come pick me up from school again today?" she asked.

"Sure," he said. "I don't think I can park in the church lot, though, so expect me to be directly outside the school."

"That's fine. The only reason I wanted you to park there was so you wouldn't see what a loser I am. That ship has already sailed."

"You aren't a loser, Katie," he said. "Not even close."

He had to drag his eyes away as she finally stood up and bent over to open the bottom drawer of her dresser. Her butt was small, but spectacular, pale and perfectly slappable. He wanted to slap himself for the thought as willed his legs to exit her room.

CHAPTER 15

Rebecca was downstairs when Jake returned to the kitchen, wearing a bathrobe and still messy from sleep. She was cooking breakfast, pancakes and eggs and bacon, and listening to an audiobook on her phone's speaker.

"No work today?" asked Jake.

"I usually take Fridays off or do my appointments online," said Rebecca. "I plan on taking a bath and kicking my weekend off early."

"Sounds like fun," said Jake. "Breakfast smells incredible."

"Thanks, sweetie."

Kate came down a few minutes later, dressed for school but still moving slowly and rubbing her forehead.

"Are you okay, Kate?" asked Rebecca.

"Fine," she muttered. "Just tired. Too much homework last night."

"You sure?" asked Rebecca. "You seem a little under the weather."

"Maybe it was something she ate," suggested Jaimie. "Or drank."

Rebecca looked perplexed. Kate scowled at her sister. Jake focused on the food as his mother set a plate down in front of him. Kate gave him a hug and reminded him to pick her up as she left, getting a ride from Jaimie, who was headed to an early morning yoga class she'd been taking at the local gym.

He finished eating. His mother went upstairs, and for a while, he just sat and aimlessly considered what to do for the day. He'd forgotten about the remote in the drama of Kate's bullying. He made his way up to his room, found the remote, and tossed a pair of the new batteries into it.

Nothing happened when he hit the power button. There was a tiny LED that he supposed would flick on if it was working correctly. If the remote was busted, it would be far harder to track the toy down, lacking any way of turning it on to alert him to its presence. He considered if perhaps he could bring it somewhere to fix it.

Lorenzo had seemed helpful and perhaps capable of such a task, but again, Jake wondered if he needed to be discrete about how he proceeded. He considered finding a sex toy store in the area, if one existed, and seeing what advice they might have. He could at least be more at ease about his secrecy dealing with professionals.

"Jake?" His mother's voice came from across the hall, in the upstairs bathroom.

"Yeah Mom?"

"Can you grab me a towel? I forgot to bring a clean one in with me."

"Sure," he said. "Downstairs in the laundry room, right?"

"Exactly."

He went down, grabbed a clean towel, and came back up. Pausing at the door to the bathroom, he opened it partially and thrust his arm with the towel through.

"Here."

"I'm in the bath," said his mother. "Bring it in and put it down where I can reach it."

He opened the door further, hearing the sound of the audiobook she'd been listening to before. She'd lit a couple of scented candles, and the air was steamy and fragrant. His eyes briefly tracked across the tub and the very naked woman within it.

Most of his mother's body was obscured by the bubbles, but that somehow made the sight of her that much more lurid. He could make out the shape of her breasts, large and wet and slick, and the hint of her nipples. Her arms were resting outside the tub on the porcelain edge, the left one rising as he offered her the towel.

"Thanks Jake," said Rebecca. "Can you do one more quick favor for me?"

He was frozen, unable to do anything but stare at her. She looked so different with her glasses off — strange to think that with so much else on display. He wished he could see her nipples properly through the bubbles and felt a sudden, compelling stirring in his loins.

"Jake?" said his mother.

"Sorry, what was that?"

"I want to clip my nails but I left my nail clipper in my room." She gave him a patient and somewhat knowing smile, perhaps at least partially aware of the effect she was having on him. "Can you get them for me?"

"Absolutely." He turned away from her with stiff motions and left the bathroom, feeling himself escaping the heat of the steam and the situation.

He realized that he hadn't asked her where she kept her nail clippers as he entered her room, but also that it provided him with an opportunity. It was the perfect excuse to rifle around a little bit, see if there was anything in one of her drawers that she might want kept out of sight. It seemed incredibly unlikely that the Master Pulse belonged to his mother, but still...

He went to her dresser first, pulling it open carefully and quietly. Rebecca was still listening to her audiobook, giving him assurance that he'd hear it turn off or come closer if she did climb out of the bath. Most of the top drawer was socks, underwear, and bras. Jake felt his face heat up as he prodded around a bit, moving stuff aside.

There was something else, an item that jumped out at him and was damning in its own right. A pair of pink fuzzy handcuffs, the kind intended for play. The kind intended for... sex play. He felt short of breath, blood rushing to his head and another conspicuous place.

The image of his mother on her back on her bed came to mind, hands handcuffed to her headboard, rubbing her thighs together and gasping as the different levels of the Magic Pulse were tested one by one.

"Jake?" called Rebecca. "You didn't forget, did you? They should be on my dresser."

"I see them," he called, quietly closing the top drawer.

He grabbed the nail clippers and brought them back to the bathroom, adjusting himself before he entered to at least downplay his arousal a little.

"Thanks sweetie," said Rebecca.

"No problem, Mom."

He brought them over and set them on the edge of the bath, the image of her nude in the tub with less bubbles concealing her body than ever creeping in at the corner of his vision.

Jake returned to his room, closed the door, and took out the remote. He tried again to get it to turn on to no avail. Part of him wondered if he could simply put the matter to rest, having seen what he'd seen. The Magic Pulse had to be his mother's. At the very least, she was now his prime suspect.

Except he hadn't actually found the toy itself. It was possible that the kinkiness was coming from multiple places within the house. He wondered why he cared so much, but it was a question that didn't have an answer in words, but in a deeper stirring.

CHAPTER 16

Jake spent most of the morning and the afternoon shadow boxing with his arousal. He wanted to simply watch porn and rub one out, but each time he sat down with the intention of doing so, his mind pulled him in directions he didn't want to go in. It felt like watching any of the copious amounts of porn targeted at people with similar taboo attractions would only cement his perversions into permanence.

He knew he was probably being overdramatic. It was less about a fear of being tainted and more of the fear of being caught, he supposed. His mother would probably have a mostly open mind, as a therapist. Jaimie would torment him and never let him live it down. Kate would...

Fuck. Kate. He looked at the clock and realized he'd whiled away the day. If he wanted to be on time to pick her up, he needed to get moving.

He hurried downstairs and grabbed his keys. Rebecca was sitting at the kitchen table, still listening to her audiobook with her laptop open. She waved to him and blew a kiss as he hurried over to the front door.

"Ride safe," she said.

"I will. Enjoy your audiobook."

She smiled and nodded. The section of the book currently playing featured two characters flirting dangerously with one another and he couldn't help but notice how flushed his mother's cheeks were.

He put on his helmet and wheeled his bike out of the garage. He made sure the second helmet was in the cargo net for Katie, started it up, and set off.

The cold air on his face had a sobering effect on his mood and outlook. He was spending too much time at home, in the house. That was the real issue - sheer proximity to three gorgeous, intelligent, and potentially sexually devious women.

He needed to get a job and make some new friends. A girlfriend, specifically. Someone who could hold his attention, if not entirely outcompete the moments that created those little illicit impulses to begin with.

He was running a little late to pick up Kate and had to speed a bit to make it on time. A long line of cars was already queued in the pickup lane and he took his place at the end, slowly waddling his bike forward as each one took a generous amount of time picking up their teenage charge.

He took off his helmet right before it was his turn on the strip. Kate appeared outside the school's front doors after a minute or so. He'd expected to see her similarly distraught to how she'd been the previous day and was ready to swoop in if needed to forcibly chase off her bullies. With Kate, he at least felt honorable, like a proper big brother defending her as needed and as appropriate.

She was walking with somebody, not one of the girls from the previous day as far as Jake could tell, but another senior with a blonde braid and sunglasses. Kate waved to the girl as she walked off, laughing at something she said and looking uncertainly toward Jake. He got off the bike to get Kate's helmet for her as she ran over to him.

"Hey!" she called.

She wrapped her arms around him, hugging him tightly, and then kissed him... on the lips. He was so surprised that he could only kiss her back, holding her body against his, tasting fruit flavored lip balm. He blinked as the kiss ended and he let his arms fall away from his sister's body.

"Come on," she said. "You're bringing me home, right?"

Kate's eyes seemed to plead with him to not say anything, not make a scene. He nodded and climbed onto the bike, pulling his helmet on, still with the taste of her fresh on his lips. Kate climbed on behind him as they pulled out of the school's driveway and onto the road.

He didn't take her home right away. He stopped at a gas station, more to talk than to fill up. Kate wouldn't meet his gaze as they both took off their helmets and stood next to the bike.

"Katie," he said. "What's going on? Why did you... do that?"

She shrugged. "I don't know."

"Hey." He touched her shoulders and waited until she looked at him. "I'm not mad. I think I can guess part of it, at least. Just talk to me."

"I'm sorry," she muttered. "I just... Can this wait until we get home?"

"Yeah, I suppose it can."

He did end up throwing some gas in his bike before they rode the rest of the way home. Rebecca was still in the kitchen, laptop out but audiobook silent. Jaimie was on the couch, dressed in her workout clothes and munching on an apple.

"Thanks for picking Kate up again, Jake," said Rebecca. "Do either of you want a snack before dinner? I had Jaimie buy some fruit from the grocery store while she was out with my car."

Jake was still focused on the situation with Kate, but did his best to act normal. "Jaimie ran an errand for you? What did you have to bribe her with to make that happen?"

"Hey!" called Jaimie. "That's so unfair."

"The leftover change from the money I gave her," said Rebecca.

"I'm not hungry," said Kate. "I have some homework I need to get done. Jake, can you still help me with it?"

"Yeah, for a little bit," he said.

"Aw," said Jaimie. "Jakey-kun is not only picking up his little sister, but helping her with homework. What did she have to bribe you with to make that happen?"

"As it happens, all she had to do was be a chill sister," said Jake. "You should try it sometime."

He followed Kate up to her room. She let him enter first, closed the door behind her, and then locked it.

"Jeez," said Jake. "I see security is tight today."

Kate went over to her computer and put on some music, not loud, but loud enough to obscure their voices even if someone was listening right outside the door.

"I just don't want Jaimie finding out about this. Or Mom."

"Why'd you do it in the first place, Katie?" He sat down on her bed and looked at her seriously. "Why'd you kiss me?"

Kate took a seat next to him and stared down at the bed for a few seconds. "Did you see the girl that I was with when I left school today?"

"The blonde one with the braid?"

She nodded. "That's my friend, Amber. My only friend, really. She got in with the popular kids when we were freshman, but she wasn't part of the bullying and the fake instagram. She wasn't like my best friend or anything, but she always acknowledged and was always nice. Maybe that is a best friend when you're as much of a loser as I am. I don't know."

Jake put an arm around her shoulders. "I think I get it."

"She saw me when you picked me up yesterday," said Kate. "She asked if it was my boyfriend in the hall and some of the girls who hate me overheard her. Everybody was making jokes about how I finally had a real, live boyfriend all day, and, and... it's just so unfair!"

She looked up at Jake with tears in her eyes.

"Oh, Katie." He pulled her closer, into a side hug.

"I just shouted back at one of them that of course I have a boyfriend, and of course he doesn't go to this school. I said I'd... never date any of the jerks from my school, and that's basically true. Part of me enjoyed lying to them. They tortured me with that fake instagram boyfriend. It just felt... fair, you know? To fake a boyfriend just like they did to me. Maybe not fair, but like I was taking some of my power back."

"Hey, if it made you feel better than no harm done," said Jake. "Especially given that I didn't go to your school and nobody there knows me. Hard to disprove."

"So you don't mind?"

"Not really," he said. "Not for you."

"Even if I have to kiss you again when you pick me up from now on?"

He blinked, surprised by the question and how it excited him in a strange way. "A kiss every now and then is... no big deal, I suppose."

"I also kind of said that, you know, since it's a Friday night, that maybe..." Kate trailed off into quiet mumbling. "...I'd go on a double date with Amber and her boyfriend Trevor. With my boyfriend."

She looked up at him with pleading eyes, so fragile and innocent.

"Oh, Katie," he said, shaking his head reflexively. "That might be... a little trickier."

She blinked a few times, moisture encroaching into the corners of her eyes. One of her hands touched his, squeezing with soft desperation.

"Fine," he said. "Whatever. Just for tonight."

"Yay! Thanks Jake!" She kissed him on the cheek, distraught mood discarded like a used piece of bubble gum. "We're going to the movies. We have to be there by seven so you should start getting ready around five."

She stood up and went over to her dresser, all but ignoring him as she started picking an outfit. Jake frowned and silently reassessed his view of his quiet and delicate little sister.

CHAPTER 17

Jake showered, shaved, and put on a button-down shirt with a nice, newish pair of jeans. Kate hadn't mentioned dinner being part of the date, so he nibbled on some of the fruit his mother had gotten Jaimie to buy. He actually preferred no dinner, given how it would involve sitting down and talking — lying — about his and Kate's relationship for an extended period of time.

There would still be lying involved. The entire thing was a complete charade, but one he would dutifully play if it meant helping his little sister regain some of her lost social status.

Jaimie was downstairs when Jake came into the kitchen. She smirked as though she'd just smelled something rotten and pointed at him.

"Looking fancy there, Jakey-kun." She walked up close to him and adjusted one of his shirt buttons, hands moving up to fiddle with his collar afterward. "You got a date tonight or something?"

"No," he said, a touch too quickly. "I'm... getting drinks with an old buddy of mine from high school."

"Tell me you aren't planning on riding your bike home afterward," called Rebecca, from the kitchen.

"I promise I'll call you for a ride if I end up having more than one," he said.

"Thanks, sweetie," said Rebecca. "Please do."

He got a text from Kate as he munched on an apple.

Pick me up at the end of the block near the house with the metal fence

Sighing, Jake wondered if giving in to Kate's request might have been a mistake. He waited until 6:30 before texting Kate back, letting her know he'd be waiting at the spot in a few minutes. After saying a quick goodbye to his mom and Jaimie, he set out. It was dark, but he picked out Kate easily enough as she made her way after him a short time later.

She looked unbelievable, his little sister transformed into a teenage beauty. She wore a black dress with a floral print with a white sweater over top that emphasized her modest bust and petite build. Her red hair hung loose across her shoulders, and her makeup was expertly applied to accentuate her innate cuteness and freckles.

"Kate," he muttered, climbing off the bike to hug her as she approached. "Wow."

"You think it's okay?" She blushed and did a twirl. "It's been a while since I last dressed up."

"It's more than okay, Katie," he said. "It's..."

Incredible. Sexy. Hot in a way that makes me imagine all the movements it would take to unwrap you and strip you naked.

"...perfect," he finished.

Kate's smile was genuine and brilliant. Jake climbed onto his bike, heart racing as his sister's arms and body pressed against him from behind. He set it into gear and set off for the theater with a fair amount of time to spare.

Amber and Trevor were already waiting outside the theater, leaning against a lamppost at the edge of the sidewalk with playful body language toward one another. Trevor was tall and broad shouldered, though not quite conventionally handsome with more of a block for a face. Amber had dressed up and looked like a fairly typical teenage girl on a date, blonde and pretty.

Jake parked his bike and climbed off. Kate fussed over her helmet as she took it off, obviously worried about messing up her hair. Jake smiled at her, more as a brother than a pretend boyfriend.

"You still look fine," he said. "Don't worry."

"I'm so nervous," she muttered.

"Hey, you're supposed to be on a date with me, not Amber," he said. "Come on."

Kate giggled and took his hand. Amber and Trevor came over to them, expressions friendly and curious. Jake noticed and felt somewhat wary of the way Trevor's eyes scanned over Kate's figure as they drew closer.

"Kate!" said Amber. "I'm so glad you could make it. This is your new boyfriend, I take it?"

"Jake," said Jake. "Nice to meet you."

"Jake, this is Trevor," said Amber. "Trevor, Jake."

Trevor nodded in greeting. Amber and Kate hugged briefly, the blonde girl leaning in close to whisper something out of earshot. Kate giggled and nodded, blushing. Jake and Trevor watched awkwardly, sharing a glance that silently asked the other if they had a clue what their respective dates were up to.

"We're going to see Lost Cause, that new horror movie," said Amber. "The two of you don't scare easy, do you?"

"Of course not!" snapped Kate.

Jake nodded, but he was well aware that scary movies had always terrified his little sister, not just as a kid but well into her teenage years.

"You sure, Katie?" he asked.

"It's fine," she said.

"I've been dying to see this movie," said Trevor. "It's gotten bad reviews but who cares, right? The trailer looked crazy fucking awesome."

"You're such a boy," whispered Amber.

"Sorry babe," said Trevor.

Jake was somewhere in between liking and disliking Kate's bestie and her meathead boyfriend, but they weren't why he was there. "We'll get some popcorn and soda, then. Set up with snacks and have a fun night."

He took Kate's hand and held it, finding it strangely easy to sink into the role of her boyfriend. He cared about her at least as much as a boyfriend would. He wanted her to have fun. She was smiling and he felt like he was on the right track.

They entered the theater and paid for their tickets. Jake got in line for snacks alongside Trevor. He watched Kate laughing with Amber, the two of them seeming like genuine friends. It felt so different from seeing her quiet side at home, or the way she'd guarded and sealed herself off against the bullying at school.

"We're going to grab seats," said Kate. "We'll aim for the center row. Come find us after?"

"Of course," said Jake.

She darted forward and kissed him on the lips. Jake felt a wave of heat rush through him as he watched her hurry off after Amber.

"She's a hot little piece of ass." Trevor made a whistling noise accompanied by poking his index finger into the mostly closed fingers of his other hand. "Have the two of you, like, you know. Fucked yet?"

"Spencer," said Jake. "That is none of your business."

"Trevor."

"Whatever."

CHAPTER 18

Jake made a bit of friendly small talk with his counterpart to ease the tension of being on a double date with a blonde and a blockhead. When he and Trevor finally did make their way into the theater to find Kate and Amber, it didn't take long. They'd attracted some attention of the unwanted male variety, which was hardly a surprise given how they looked.

Jake walked up to a handsome tanned young man who was sitting behind Kate, leaned forward almost completely over his seat as he whispered something to her. She was making a face as though the situation was mostly awkward, but with a touch of the same despair he'd seen in her during the bullying.

"You're going to want to find a seat elsewhere, buddy," said Jake, as he sidled past Amber and took a seat next to Kate. "She's with me."

He set a hand down on his date's knee, his... little sister's knee. The other guy's eyebrows shot up.

"I thought she was just trying to wave me off by saying she had a boyfriend," he said. "Girls lie about that stuff a lot you know."

Amber let out a small chuckle. Trevor was dealing with the other guy who'd been drawn to Amber, talking with lots of gestures that seemed more placating than threatening.

"Go ply your wares on a different street," said Jake. "Seriously. Fuck off."

"Fine, whatever. No need to go all ape man on me."

Jake's fingers tightened on Kate's knee reflexively. She made a noise, not quite a sigh, but not quite a moan. He looked over at her and saw her biting her lower lip.

"Thanks," she whispered.

"No prob." He leaned in with a conspiratorial smile. "Isn't that what boyfriends are for?"

"Well..." She smiled back at him. "That's not all they're for."

Trevor managed to ward off the other booty raider and find his seat a minute later, just as the lights dimmed. Jake never took his hand off Kate's knee. He wasn't sure why, himself. He just had this odd feeling that if he moved his hand, he'd need an excuse to put it back there, whereas if he kept it there, he could have it there for the entire movie.

On her knee, and anything else it happened to be attached to.

He was getting a little excited and knew how fucked up it was. He offered Kate some popcorn with his other hand. She took a few kernels and ate them slowly, watching him. The trailers started as Kate reached for more. It felt like the punchline of an old joke as her fingers missed the bag and felt around along his thigh in search of it, grazing his hardening cock at one point.

He rubbed a little higher up from her knee, unsure of what game his little sister was playing but intent on hitting the ball back. She let out a small, barely audible gasp, and then settled her hand more confidently on his thigh, the tip of her little finger just barely resting on the head of his hardening cock.

There was no way she couldn't feel it. He slid his own hand a little further up, taking a possessive hold on the inside of her leg. That was about as far as he could go without hiking her dress up. He instantly corrected himself. That was about as far as he could go without losing his fucking mind, as her brother.

The trailers ended and the movie started, the speakers creating an ambience of roaring sound and deafening silence. Kate kept her hand in the same place, fingers shifting or tightening alongside the tension and scares. Jake wanted to see what would happen if he simply took hold of her wrist and shifted her touch up a few inches, right on to his now stiff erection.

He shook the thought away even as he started rubbing along Kate's thigh with his own hand. She made a little noise and he couldn't resist teasing her a bit. He leaned in close.

"Enjoying the movie, Katie?" he whispered.

"Yeah," she whispered back. "I am."

He rubbed some more and heard her let out a shuddering exhale. Her own hand briefly shifted down, running one time along the full length of his cock, the sensation vivid and blissful even through the thick denim of his jeans. But that was all she risked, all she had confidence for, or perhaps that was simply where her line was.

He wanted more, and he hated that he wanted more. He wanted to kiss her, to tease her. He wanted her in a way he wasn't sure he'd ever wanted Estelle or Asa, which only made his guilt and shame all the more profound. He wasn't supposed to want her. He couldn't have her. It was all pretend, and somehow that only made it that much more exciting.

The movie seemed to fly by and Jake felt a strange sense of disappointment when it reached the end. The lights came back on. Kate pulled her hand away as though afraid of getting caught. He took his off her thigh more slowly, watching her as he did so.

"What'd you think?" he asked.

"I liked it," she whispered. "I'd watch the sequel."

"Would you?"

He smiled and leaned in a little closer, feeling like a bastard, but unable to resist. Kate smirked back, the same mischievous one he'd seen before.

He kissed her and felt her lips moving back hungrily against his. He risked going deeper, tongue flirting into her mouth. Amber laughed from further down the aisle and the spell was broken.

"We were going to hang out in the park across the street," she said, sounding drunk. "Still have some left. The two of you are welcome to join us."

She showed off a half-full bottle of vodka that had apparently been in her purse. Jake looked at Kate.

"I... want to hang out for a bit, if that's okay," she said. "I don't really want the night to be over just yet."

"I'm right there with you, Katie."

He touched her thigh one last time and her eyes did this insanely hot fluttering thing. He had to adjust himself as he stood up to make his hard on less obvious. The people nearer to the end of the aisle weren't moving yet, and had to crowd in close behind Kate. He touched her hips, feeling an urge to have her against him, to grind into her. He resisted.

Stop this, he thought. You're taking it too far. She's your little sister.

The lights in the theater's lobby helped him calm down, returning a sense of normalcy and rules to his reality. Amber and Trevor's drunken laughter and boisterousness helped in much the same way. They left the theater and started walking to the park. The moon was out and it was one of those unseasonably warm fall nights, wind blowing fallen leaves across the street with a soft rattle.

"Race you to the swings!"

Amber let out a whoop and took off ahead of the rest of them. Trevor followed close behind. Jake exchanged a look with Kate and kept his normal walking pace.

When they caught up, Trevor was sitting on one of the swings with Amber on his lap, blushing and smiling. It didn't appear like anything more was going on, but that was enough in itself. They rocked back and forth with gentle motions, the childishness of the swing made somehow lewd by their positions atop it.

"Kate!" called Amber. "Catch!"

She tossed the vodka bottle at Kate. Jake caught it for her, knowing that his little sister had never been a master of hand-to-eye coordination. She whispered "thanks" and gently took it from his hand, taking a deep swig.

"Go easy," he said.

"I'm..." She broke off into a small coughing fit. "...getting a ride home from you, remember?"

She set the bottle down next to Amber's purse and eyed the swing. Jake walked over to it slowly and sat down, watching Kate, letting her decide what to do. She took small steps toward him, smoothed out her dress underneath him, and sank down into his lap.

Instantly, his cock began to stir. Kate held on to the swing's chains, but Jake still wrapped an arm around her waist. They didn't swing all that fast, mimicking the way Trevor and Amber rocked back and forth. It shifted Kate on his crotch, her soft butt seeming to draw all the blood he had straight to his member.

Kate was breathing faster, little sounds coming out with each swing forward. Jake couldn't tell if Amber and Trevor were watching them or not. He didn't really care, either way. He slid his hand up the front of Kate's body. Even though he was directly in control of the movement, he still felt surprise when his palm suddenly cupped her breast.

"Oh," whispered Kate.

She started rocking her hips, grinding her soft little butt against his hard cock. Jake touched her more freely, rocking the swing back in forth in a way that felt almost like fucking with clothes on.

From the corner of his eye, he saw Amber lean forward off the swing and seemingly take her panties off. Trevor was doing something with his pants. It was hard to see in the dark exactly what, but Jake suspected he knew.

"You guys don't mind, do you?" asked Amber. "We could always go to Trev's car but we'd probably just call it a night."

"One advantage of a car over a bike, right?" laughed Trevor.

"Kate doesn't mind." Jake started pulling her skirt up, intent on at least getting a hand into her panties. "Right, Katie?"

"I... don't mind."

She was breathing fast as Jake began rubbing her crotch through her panties. He was seeing and thinking through a haze of lust. He knew how wrong it all was, but couldn't stop. Didn't want to stop. She could stop him. Why didn't she?

Amber let out a wavering, erotic moan. Trevor made a grunting noise, and the sounds of the chains of the other swing sounded more like the two were bouncing rather than swaying. Jake took hold of Kate's hips with one hand and rocked her back and forth as he continued to molest her through her panties. She leaned back against him, breath fluttering, the motion of her body urgent.

A ring tone sounded from Kate's purse. She swore under her breath and stood up, hurrying to grab it. Jake saw her frown by the light of the display and knew what she was about to say.

"It's Mom." She blinked once, perhaps realizing her phrasing. "My mom, I mean."

Amber and Trevor didn't seem to be listening. Jake stood up, still horny but aware of what would happen if Kate stayed out too late.

"I think I... better get her home safe," he said, reluctantly.

Trevor and Amber were still engaged with each other and Jake was interested in getting their attention if it meant having to see what they were doing. He put an arm around Kate and began walking her toward his bike.

CHAPTER 19

The ride home was pleasant and uneventful. Jake opened the garage door and parked his bike. Kate got off and handed him the second helmet, smiling and standing as though she was starting to feel the vodka from earlier.

"That was fun," she said, quietly.

"Yeah, it wasn't bad."

Jake scratched his neck, feeling awkward. He'd gone so much further with her than he'd planned. This was the moment where he expected she'd call him out.

"I've never been on a real date before," said Kate. "Well, outside of middle school and that doesn't really count."

"I'm glad you had fun, Katie," he said.

But it was all just pretend, he wanted to add. He didn't say it.

"I had more than just fun, Jake," she said, with a dangerous smile. "Do I get a kiss goodnight?"

He hesitated, and opened his mouth fully intending to draw a hard boundary. "I did promise to get you home safe."

He stepped in close, set a hand on her hip, and kissed her. Kate pressed herself against him so quickly that it almost felt like they were back in the park, grinding on the swing, listening to Amber and Trevor possibly fucking brazenly alongside them. Jake reached down to grope his little sister's soft butt. He wanted to feel it against his cock again. Feel more than just that.

The door connecting the garage to the living room suddenly swung open. Jake parted from Kate in a swift movement but knew how guilty he must have looked in the aftermath. Jaimie stood on the step in a workout bra and sweatpants, frowning at them.

"Jesus Christ," said Jaimie. "I thought someone had broken in! What the fuck are you two doing out here?"

"Nothing!" said Kate, way too quickly and vehemently.

"Kate... had a rough night," he said, a bit more smoothly. "She called me for a ride home. She's been drinking a little."

Jaimie folded her arms. "You dropped everything and rushed out to bring Kate home just because she was having a bad night?"

"Yeah, I did." He looked right at Jaimie, daring her to call his bluff. "She's my sister. I'd do the same for you if you weren't so grumpy toward me all the time."

"Asshole. But good work." Jaimie sighed and looked at Kate. "You are going to end up on a bad path if you keep drinking so much, Kate."

"I know my limits," she muttered.

"Yeah, but the guys who are going to start giving you attention won't respect said limits," said Jaimie. "Trust me on that."

Kate glanced at Jake, and he interpreted the foreign look he saw in her eyes.

"They'll have to go through her big brother, first," he said.

"Sure they will, John Wick," said Jaimie, with healthy skepticism. "Now come on. Mom's going to wake up and catch you out here if you don't get inside soon."

Jake and Kate were mostly silent as they took off their shoes and padded upstairs. Jaimie was still down in the living room, and they had a moment in the hallway as they were about to retire to their respective rooms.

"Thanks Jake," whispered Kate.

She looked at him with a tiny smile and waited a few seconds. He wanted to kiss her again and could tell she wanted it, too. The current of tension between them all but demanded it, but that only seemed to make it more critical that he resist. They were inside the family home, with their mother sleeping in her room across the other side of a door, Jaimie capable of stumbling up on them at any second.

"Sleep tight," he whispered.

He pulled away from her, slipped into his room, and closed the door with a force of effort. It was hard to know whether he'd done right or wrong across the span of the night, but he was at least happy that he'd made Kate happy.

***

Jake realized as he woke up the next morning that something was a little bit off. His bed felt like there was someone else on it. He let out a sleepy groan and rolled from his stomach onto his side, feeling his morning wood popping loose with stubborn energy. He'd slept in just his boxers, obviously not expecting company.

Kate was laying next to him, wearing one of her girlie pink nightgowns that she'd had since she was twelve, one of the ones that barely even fit her anymore. He watched her, eyes still half lidded, and saw her smile and blush.

"Good morning," she whispered. "I came to wake you up. Mom's already downstairs making waffles and coffee cake. She does a big breakfast on the weekend."

"That so?" He cleared his throat and blinked his eyes further open. "Well, then it is a good morning."

Kate giggled and looked like she was fighting a bigger smile than the one she already had on. Her eyes drifted down from his face and Jake felt a rush of heat as he sensed her gaze taking in his incredibly obvious boner.

"It must suck being a guy," she said, voice quiet.

"Not as much as you'd think." He slid a little closer to her, unable to help himself.

"No?" Kate finally let her smile blossom and leaned her face closer to his. "What makes it fun, then?"

He at least had the self-control not to kiss her on the lips. It hardly mattered. He felt her quiver as his lips touched her cheek. He pulled her closer to him, letting his erection prod against her upper thigh. Kate let out a nervous, fluttering laugh that bit off into a quiet moan. She hugged herself against him and kissed him several times on the cheek, apparently drawing the same line.

"This is nice," she whispered.

One of her legs lifted to drape over his. She probably thought it was cute. Jake could feel how dangerous the situation was. He was still fogged over from sleep, still so fucking horny from sleep. The last thing he needed to start his Saturday off was fucking his little sister sticky and senseless. Or was that exactly what the morning called for?

"Kate," he said, mustering his older brother authority. "I have to wake up now."

"That's what I came to help you do," she giggled. "Mission accomplished, I suppose."

She leaned in to kiss him again, eyes taking on a dangerous gleam as she pressed her lips against his instead of opting for the cheek. It was like shooting the starting pistol as Jake kissed her back intensely and the moment began spiraling into madness. Jake wondered if Kate even knew herself what she'd been doing, why she'd been drawn to him. Where it would lead.

For a span of three to five seconds, they were kissing and groping each other with the reckless abandon of horny youth. He got a full hold of one of her breasts as he shifted to kissing her neck. He came to his senses as he started to roll her onto her back, footsteps from either Jaimie or his mother passing down the hallway and making them both freeze.

"Seriously," he said, coming to his senses. "I need to get dressed."

"I know." She rolled off his bed over one shoulder in the ultimate cute little sister fashion, flashing her white panties in the process. "Hang out with me today? I need help."

"On what?"

"My computer again, I think," she said. "Please?"

I need to get better at saying no to her, he thought. Fast.

"Sure," he said. "After breakfast, though."

And after rubbing out his morning wood. The temptation was becoming far too much for him to handle.

"Yes!" She grinned and did a little dance on her way to the door. "Thanks, Jake."

CHAPTER 20

Jake never managed to get the relief he sought. He was still in the process of picking out his porn when his mother called him down for breakfast, emphasizing that it was her "special weekend buffet."

The smell was incredible before he even saw the food. Rebecca had made a big coffee cake, waffles, a platter of cut fruit, home fries with little bits of bacon mixed in, along with eggs and toast. She had on a silk kimono, black and pink with floral print, and it left precious little to the imagination.

Kate was still in her tiny nightgown. Jaimie had on a baggy t-shirt and shiny nylon boy shorts. Jake really wished he'd taken an extra five minutes to expel all the nasty thoughts and urges from his body. He took a breath and exhaled it as he sat down, willing the blood to more productive places in his body.

Rebecca smiled at him from across the table. "It's so nice having you home for the weekend, Jake. Any plans for your first Saturday back?"

Jaimie scoffed as she stabbed a waffle with her fork. "As though he's cool enough to have weekend plans. Something tells me he will spend most of it alone in his room."

Jake shot his sister an irritated look. "Fuck off, Jaimie. I'm helping Kate with her computer again, to start."

"That's nice of you!" said their mother.

She stood up to grab the coffee pot, the sash of her kimono coming loose. Jake caught a glimpse of cleavage as she leaned over the table to refill his mug. He quickly looked away, shifting again.

"Thanks, Jake," Kate said quietly next to him. "I don't need that much help. Just enough to get it back online."

Jaimie let out an exaggerated yawn as she grabbed a piece of bacon off the platter. "So Jakey-kun. Why do you look so tired this morning? What exactly happened to you last night, anyway?"

"Nothing happened," he said, a little too quickly. "I just hung out with a friend and then gave Kate a ride."

Jaimie looked at Kate next.

"Same," said Kate. "Except I got a ride from Jake instead."

"Did you have fun?" asked Rebecca.

"Yeah," said Kate. "I saw a movie. Hung out at the park with Amber and her boyfriend afterwards."

"Alright," said Rebecca. "I feel like I might be missing a piece of the story."

"That's because you probably are," said Jaimie with a smirk. "Pass the syrup, brother dearest."

Jake sighed as he reached across to hand her the bottle. Jaimie was irritating him with her questions and insinuations, but the way her nipples showed through her thin t-shirt made it shockingly hard to be mad at her.

Rebecca sat back down, the neckline of her kimono dipping low. "So, besides computer help, anything else fun planned?"

Jake tried to keep his eyes on his plate. "Uh, not really. Might go for a motorcycle ride later, but that's it."

"You should take Kate with you," Jaimie teased. "She seems to love riding on the back of your bike."

Kate nearly choked on her orange juice.

"Shut up," she sputtered, her cheeks turning red.

Jake winced. Jaimie's comment had barely been a barb, though he supposed there was an aspect to the vibrations of a motorcycle that she might have been teasing Kate about. He remembered the remote, the vibrator potentially hidden in some dark drawer or far closet corner within their ostensibly normal household. He remembered the fuzzy handcuffs, and in that moment, his mother smiled at him.

"More bacon, sweetie?" offered Rebecca. She had stood up again to refresh plates and refill drinks.

"Sure, thanks Mom," Jake said, trying not to stare as she leaned over him.

Having her so close was even worse after everything he'd done with Kate the night before and almost done that morning. Was this how criminals after their first major score? As though every unlocked door and open car window represented a new opportunity, a new temptation?

He focused on the food and eating and kept his eyes mostly on his plate. He helped his mother with the dishes after everyone had finished eating. Kate lingered in the living room watching TV, while Jaimie left to go do whatever it was she did most days. Jake still didn't know.

"Ready?" asked Kate.

She had a smile on her face that brought Jake back to the previous night.

"It's probably the same problem it had before," he said.

"I still want you to help me," she said. "Come on."

She took his hand and led him up to her room. Their mother was presumably downstairs, practicing yoga or perhaps or having a workout. He noted how Kate closed the door to her room as soon as they were in, still smiling. She'd changed into sweatpants and a tank top and brushed by him on the way to her desk.

"Nothing's loading," she said, clicking the mouse as she tried to bring up a YouTube video. "Can you do whatever you did before?"

She stayed right where she was, and Jake felt the tension rising as he thought about what he'd done before. He hadn't even been pretending to be her boyfriend, and the touch of their bodies as he'd stood behind her had been a wild turn-on. Now, they'd gone a little bit further, but seeing her half bent over at her desk, butt jutting out just right, felt like too much of an invitation.

"Let me get in there and see what I can do."

Jake came up behind her, acutely aware of her bare shoulders, the way her tank top hugged her breasts, but most of all, her smell. She was a little musky from sleep, but with hints of the deodorant she'd worn the night before.

He moved with deliberate slowness as he reached around her for the mouse, letting his crotch briefly brush against her ass. Kate let out a soft exhale, arching into him.

"I'll try the obvious stuff first," he said, leaning in close, talking low.

He felt his cock growing hard at the speed of dark magic. There was no way she couldn't feel it. The fact that he knew she could feel it, stubbornly pressed against her soft, sweet butt, was even more of a turn on.

"Try whatever you want to," whispered Kate.

She had to know how that sounded. She had to know what she was saying. Jake set a hand on her hip and rocked against her, so turned on that he had to breathe to keep from blowing his load just from that first dry thrust against the softness of her rear.

"It's your computer, Katie," he whispered. "I don't want to just do stuff without permission."

"I trust you, Jake." She flexed her buttocks and pushed back against his motions. "Whatever you need to do."

He let go of the mouse and ran his hands up her body, almost cupping her breasts through her flimsy tank top. "Could reset it. Would only take a sec to get it turned on again."

"Go ahead." Kate was breathing heavy, not really playing the game anymore. "Do it."

He risked it. He let his hands settle over her breasts, perfectly cuppable though not quite large. He rocked against her more dominantly. Kate whimpered as she rubbed her butt back against him. One of her hands swept the wireless mouse off the desk and it landed heavy, the bottom coming loose along with a battery.

"Oops." She let out a breathless laugh and playfully elbowed him in the ribs. "Nice one, Jake. Hope you plan on buying me a new mouse if it's broken."

He chuckled and grabbed her wrist. "That was all you, Katie. Don't think you can pout your way to getting me to pay up."

"I'll just go to Mom and tell her that you broke it on purpose."

She grinned and booped him backward with her butt. Jake still had her wrist and pulled her close again. She let out a girlish laugh and leapt onto him as though they were wrestling. And they were wrestling, straight toward and then onto her bed.

Jake felt his sense of shame and reason returning with a vengeance as he straddled Kate. She was his little sister. The moment had gotten out of hand. His hands had gotten out of hand, both of which were now tugging her tank top up, sliding over clothing and bare flesh. Kate reached up to rub his chest, biting her lower lip.

"Katie..." He sighed, still groping one of her breasts, but unable to keep any pretense up anymore. "We should stop."

"What?" she said, a little too innocently. "It's just wrestling. Just pretend. Like at the theater and on the swings."

"Until it's not." He gave her a look as she rocked her hips into him in a way that made his cock throb with pleasure. "Seriously. We're playing too close to the fire."

"Maybe I want to get burned."

"You should save those kinds of burns for a nice, honest boy," he said. "One that you'll find eventually. One that you love."

She pouted at him, still running her hands across his chest and making small grinding motions with her body. "Do you still love your exes?"

The question scalded him like acid. He didn't love either of his ex-girlfriends. In fact, the extent of his non-love was such as to make him question if he ever had loved them in the first place. But that wasn't the answer Kate needed.

"In a way." He shrugged, feeling the weakness of the lie. "Not so much anymore, but I used to."

"That's even worse," said Kate. "Maybe you should have taken your own advice."

She playfully pushed his shoulder, and then seemed to change gears, reaching down toward his crotch. Jake caught her wrist, but she smiled wickedly and tried to pull it away to continue the motion.

He pinned it above her pillow, and then suddenly they were kissing, everything more intense than before. It was like a rockslide, a slide of bodies, inexorable and needy. He squeezed her pert tits and humped into her, and then reached down intent on stripping off her sweatpants.

Footsteps sounded from the hallway. The two of them scrambled apart from one another as the spell was forcibly broken. Jake hunched over at her computer, both as a pretense for being in her room and to somewhat downplay his erection. Kate's apparently unlocked door swung open. Their mother stood on the other side, frowning.

"What's going on up here?" asked Rebecca.

"I was... helping Katie with her computer," he said.

"He broke my mouse." Kate jabbed an accusatory finger at him, clothing and hair still rumpled from their foreplay. "So I... jumped on him."

Their mother smiled and sighed. "Fair enough, I suppose. I thought... well, it doesn't matter what I thought."

"What?" Kate narrowed her eyes. "What did you think?"

"I thought you'd snuck a boy over." Rebecca shrugged. "You are seeing someone, aren't you? All the signs are there from when Jaimie first started dating."

"What? No!" Kate shook her head, but her denial melted away and she shrugged. "Well... sort of."

"Well, just be sure to give us a heads up if you do want to have him over," said Rebecca.

"Ew, Mom, don't be gross!"

Kate tossed a pillow at her and Rebecca laughed and stepped back into the hallway. Jake waited a few seconds until he heard her descend the stairs before making his own exit.

"Should be online now," he said. "I'm going to... take a shower."

"Okay." Kate waited until he started to turn away. "Jake?"

"Yeah?"

"Amber texted me about a party that's happening tonight," she said. "Asked if me and my boyfriend wanted to go."

He shook his head, sensing that it was a bad idea. "Katie..."

"Please, Jake!" She rolled onto her stomach on the bed, tank top shifting to hint at her cleavage. "I haven't been invited to a party in... well, ever, I think. Please!"

"You should go," he said. "Just not with me. There'd be too many people there. Someone might recognize me and realize what we're doing."

"Please please please?"

"I'll wait up for you here at the house, okay," he said. "Go, and if you have fun, enjoy the night. If you don't, come home and we'll watch a movie or something."

Kate made a grumbling noise and pouted at him. "...Fine. It won't be any fun without you, though. But I did already tell Amber I'd go."

"Good." He stood in her doorway, feeling a bit strange. "I'll... take my shower now."

"Have fun," she said.

CHAPTER 21

Jake's shower was lukewarm, probably from Jaimie and his mother having already gone ahead with their morning bathing. He was tempted to get himself off, but also felt an urge not to. His teasing with Kate was reaching a bursting point and part of him seemed eager to feed the flames. He knew he shouldn't, but knowing and doing were never one and the same.

He did go for a bike ride, as he'd been planning. A simple lap around town ostensibly to clear his head. It was midafternoon when he got back and Kate was getting ready for her party. Seeing her dressed in tight jeans and a flirty white top, red hair hanging in a neat braid, makeup carefully applied, was enough to fuzzy his thoughts up again.

"You're going to have fun, Katie," he said. "I mean it. Have fun."

"I will." She smiled. "I texted Amber and she sent me the address. I'm really going to go."

"I'm really encouraging you to go."

Kate crossed her arms and sat down heavily on the couch. "What happens if some guy starts flirting with me while I'm there?"

Jake felt a double flash of jealousy, as her older brother and pretend boyfriend, but was mature enough to force it down. "That's entirely up to you, Katie. Just try not to flirt with any assholes. You deserve a boyfriend who—"

"Treats me right?" she said, cutting him off. "A nice, safe boyfriend who you can beat up if he ever breaks my heart?"

"Exactly." He winked at her and felt a little better about the situation.

"I think Jaimie is going out tonight with her friends, too," said Kate. "Mom also sometimes goes dancing. You might have the place to yourself tonight."

"Possibly, yeah," he said. "I'm too boring to have plans on a Saturday night my first weekend back."

An idea came to him. If he did end up with the house to himself, it would be the perfect opportunity to search around for the Master Pulse. He'd have to be efficient about it and listen carefully in case anyone came home while he was in someone's room uninvited, but it was the best chance he might get for a while.

"Please go with me, Jake?" Kate batted her eyes at him. "I... get nervous when I think about going alone. It's all just so overwhelming, and, and, and..."

She blinked faster, but he wasn't buying it this time around.

"Feel free to work up some crocodile tears at the risk of having to redo your makeup," he said.

Kate sighed, a smile stealing onto her face. "It's not going to be as much fun without you."

"I'm flattered, but it's for the best, Katie," he said. "I'll see you later tonight."

He played video games for a while. Rebecca made nachos for dinner and he munched on a plate of them as he searched for a new sword in his video game. Kate gave him a kiss on the cheek, but didn't make another appeal for him to join her as she left to be dropped off by their mother. He felt like the fact that she couldn't ask him directly with their mom in the room only underlined his reasoning for caution.

Watching at the window as the two of them left, Jake waited until the car was around the corner at the end of the block before hurrying upstairs. He double checked that Jaimie also wasn't home before heading to his room to grab the remote.

Even with the new battery in, it still stubbornly refused to turn on, despite him alternating between tapping and holding the power button. It could have theoretically made his search much more straightforward, but even without it he still planned on seizing the opportunity he'd been handed.

Jaimie seemed like the highest priority suspect. It was hard to know for sure whether his mother or Kate would be next in line. The handcuffs had certainly put his mother on his radar, but the idea of Kate having a kinky vibrator was thrilling enough for his mind to rationalize around. It might have been a gift from her bastard of a fake e-boyfriend, even.

He started with his older sister's room. It was messy, but in a way that made sense. She had a set of string lights hung up on her wall over artwork depicting a cyberpunk geisha. A magnetic white board had a surprisingly adept doodle of half a face, or perhaps just a half finished one, feminine lips and a single eye drawn in dry erase red. Magnetic letters stuck to the board over it read "BITCH QUEEN."

Clothing was strewn everywhere. He tried opening her closet and realized it for a mistake as a rolled-up yoga mat tumbled out, along with further mess threatening to magically unsettle itself.

He put the yoga mat back and turned to her dresser and desk. The dresser was a chaotic swirl of clothing, with only a few delicate items folded and the rest just stuffed in. He didn't search deep.

The desk was more promising. He opened the top drawer and immediately found... something. He recognized the smell of weed even before he'd started rifling around. He'd smoked a fair amount in college and was fairly neutral on it. Jaimie had a vape with refillable cartridges along with a small bag of prerolled joints that were what had tipped his nose off.

He wondered where he would hide a vibrator if he were Jaimie. The answer was stupidly simple. Near the bed, probably not really hidden at all. He hesitated before moving her sheets and comforter around, but they were already disturbed from sleep and he knew she wouldn't notice.

Almost immediately he found a pair of lace panties intermingled with the mess, black with a see through patch around the upper crotch. He recoiled from them on first touch, but his disgust immediately flipped into heady intrigue.

Those were Jaimie's panties. Those were what she had on during the day, or maybe only at night. Some women put on sexy underwear just to masturbate. Estelle had told him it was what she always did, that looking sexy herself was part of her process of getting off.

It annoyed him to have that image of Jaimie in her bed, especially given how clearly he could see it. She'd strip naked, or perhaps do it fresh out of the shower, clean with the steam still clinging to her.

She'd probably let out a little moaning sigh as she slid in the Magic Pulse, and then pull the lace panties on over it. Holding the remote in one hand, she'd slowly play with the buttons, play with herself, pleasure building like a shaken-up soda until she could finally hold no more and—

The front door opened. Jake flung the panties away and quickly but silently stepped out of Jaimie's room, closing the door with utmost care. How long had he been standing there, fantasizing about his older sister? Long enough to rekindle a tragically potent erection. He tried to rearrange himself down there as he slunk back to his room.

CHAPTER 22

Jake had finally committed to finding some porn and hopefully some relief when a knock came at his door. He sighed and closed numerous browser tabs, wondering if living with three beautiful women would ever be sustainable.

"Yeah?" he called.

"It's me," said his mother. "Can I come in?"

"It's a free country."

She laughed as she opened the door. "You sound like Jaimie with that kind of answer. What's got you so frustrated tonight?"

"I'm not frustrated," he said, with a bit too much force. "I'm just... still adjusting to being home."

"I get that." Rebecca had on a maroon turtleneck sweater and dark blue chinos, baggy but in a way that only seemed to exaggerate her hips and bust. "That's kind of why I wanted to talk to you. Can we sit down for a minute?"

"Of course, Mom." He gestured to his bed and took a seat next to her as she sank down, worries rising on several fronts. "What's up?"

She looked at him for a long moment, eyes concerned and probing. "There are some boundaries which I think are needed in this household. I understand how hard it is, both from your perspective as a young man and my own as a therapist who has seen so many similar cases before."

He felt his heart sinking. She knew about him fooling around with Kate. How had they let it slip? She must have seen something or picked up on the strange new tension between them.

"I don't mind as long as it stays within certain limits," she said, reaching over to touch his knee. "You can't just go wild, Jake. A little bit from one bottle is no big deal."

"A little bit from... sorry, what?" He shook his head, mind racing to catch up. "You mean your wine?"

"Yeah..." His mother frowned. "One of the bottles I just bought has gone missing. I'm not talking about the one Kate's been sneaking from that I think she also shared with you."

Jake shook his head. "That wasn't me."

"It wasn't? Jaimie said it wasn't her and Kate doesn't usually drink that much."

"It definitely wasn't me," he said, breathing out. "I'm 21, Mom. I would just buy my own alcohol if I felt like drinking."

"Right, of course." Rebecca looked a bit embarrassed. "Sorry. I didn't mean to accuse you, honey. I can't say your denial gives me much relief. I believe you, I do. This just means that it was either Jaimie or Kate... and I think it was Kate."

"She might have brought it to share with her friends at the party," he suggested.

"And that doesn't worry you at all? The thought of her hanging out with a bunch of teenagers who, up until practically yesterday, had been ostracizing her for years?"

Jake scowled and remembered how Kate had begged him to go with her. "Isn't this healthy for her, though? She's pushing outside of her comfort zone. I thought that's the kind of thing therapists recommend."

"I'm a therapist, but I'm also her mother."

Rebecca sighed. Jake put an arm around her, surprised by how slender and feminine her shoulder felt against him.

"Can you go check up on her?" she asked. "Not right away. Maybe around eleven or a little before midnight? I want her home tonight, but I can't exactly go marching into a party to bring her back here as her mother. I think you'd have more luck as her brother, given that you're in the same age demographic."

"What happens if she doesn't want to come home?"

He winced as he put the question into words. The idea of stumbling into a party and finding Kate sloppy drunk sitting on some frat boy's lap, eager to throw her virginity away was like pouring acid into his eyes, injecting it straight into his heart. The idea of her being sober and not wanting to leave due to a newfound crush was just as bad, if not even worse.

"She'll listen to you," said Rebecca. "She's been talking to me nonstop about how much she loves having you back, Jake. We all do, but her especially. She needs you."

Jake nodded, but he wasn't sure that was such a good thing. He didn't know what he, himself, was feeling. All the lines with Katie were so blurred and tangled. He felt something for her that didn't seem quite right for a brother to be feeling.

"I'll try," he said. "Later tonight though. She needs a chance to have at least a little bit of fun."

His mother hugged him tightly. Jake felt her softness pressing into him, the swell of her breasts, the warmth of her body. He tried not to breathe in her smell, but he did it anyway, and it was intoxicating.

"Thank you, honey," she said. "Maybe I'm the one who needed you back the most."

"Well, then you've got me right where you want me."

"Oh, you can count on that."

She planted a kiss on his cheek, smiling at him with such pride. Jake smiled back, feeling an odd tension entering the moment.

"Well, I think I'll go listen to some of my audiobook," she said. "I might take another bath. I never quite know what to do with myself on the weekends."

"Have fun."

"Thanks."

She was still smiling, and Jake suddenly wished that he'd opted for searching her room more thoroughly with the chance he'd been given rather than Jaimie's.

He spent most of the evening downstairs, wondering whether Kate or Jaimie might come back early and provide him with a change of pace. His mind started wandering into places it didn't need to be.

He pictured Kate having fun, and then having too much fun. The missing bottle of wine added a dangerous undercurrent to her Saturday night outing. He wondered if he was a fool for not going with her, and then started picturing what might have happened if he'd gone with her and ended up in another gross but compelling mind space.

His mother texted him the address of where she'd dropped Kate off. Jake set out at eleven sharp, feeling a sense of urgency that he doubted was justified.

CHAPTER 23

Jake rode his motorcycle through the brisk autumn night. The address his mother had given him led him to a suburban neighborhood not far from their own, but an area he was less familiar with. The party was at a large, somewhat impressive house with a pool and lots of cars parked outside in its expansive driveway.

The music was blaring at a distance and it wasn't hard to confirm he had the right location. Jake cut the engine and dismounted his bike, feeling a sudden spike of awkwardness at how to proceed. He didn't know anyone at the party, which was, perhaps, a blessing in disguise.

A couple of pairs of teenagers were outside sitting or drinking. The front door was wide open and Jake didn't even need to announce himself as he walked in. The entrance hallway was littered with shoes, but he made the executive decision to keep his on as he noted the number of beer puddles visible at a glance. A lo-fi hip hop beat turned up too high reverberated through the house with a grumble of bass.

The living room was packed with teenagers drinking and dancing, or doing a combination of the two. Jake pushed his way through, looking for Kate or Amber or anyone else familiar. He'd been worried he might stand out, but despite him assuming it to be a high school party, there were plenty of people there who looked older, closer to his age.

It was slightly worrying, as he didn't really want to be recognized by any old acquaintances of his after having been presented to Kate's friend as her boyfriend. It would be the worst case scenario for Kate. The quicker he found her and got her home, the better.

Jake spotted Amber first. She was dancing and grinding up against a handsome, football player looking guy whose main distinct feature was not being her boyfriend, Trevor. She held up a finger to her lips as their gazes met.

Jake tried to motion for her to come over and Amber did pull away from her new hunk, but a group of teenagers stomping to a rock song which had just come on got in his way. He couldn't see where she'd disappeared to when he'd finally made his way through them.

"Hey!" said a mousey looking girl with short black hair. "I'm Frannie."

"Hi, Frannie." He forced himself to smile. "Do you know Kate? Have you seen her?"

"Kain?"

"Kate."

The girl shook her head. Jake moved past her, settling his eyes on the door that appeared to lead to the kitchen. He was stopped again, this time by a girl wearing a revealing white tank top. She had a big, beautiful smile and a body that Jake couldn't help but appreciate in a peripheral sort of way.

"You need a beer?" she asked. "Over this way."

"I'm all set. I'm looking for my..." He hesitated, unsure of how to end the sentence. "Girlfriend."

"Ah." She made a pouting face that made Jake almost share her disappointment. "That's too bad."

"Hey!" The familiar face of Trevor suddenly entered Jake's field of view. "Oh! What up Jake. You seen Amber?"

"Yeah, a minute ago," he said. "She was dancing in the living room. Have you seen Kate?"

"Uh... sort of." Trevor's face took on a pained expression. "Let me get you a beer."

"Nah, I'm good."

"I think you're going to want a beer."

Trevor clamped a hand down on Jake's shoulder, an edge of pity entering his expression. For a horrifying instant, Jake's mind flashed back to some of the more irritating and jealousy inducing scenarios he'd pictured back home on the couch.

He pushed them out of his mind. He trusted Kate. With that said, he wasn't "really" her boyfriend. He trusted her as a sister and had no claims over her due to an ill-advised make believe scenario they'd opted into for a night.

But I know her, too, he thought. I know how badly she wanted me to come to this party with her.

"You ever shotgunned a beer before?" asked Trevor.

"Unfortunately yes," he muttered. "Seriously though. I'm just looking for Kate."

Trevor handed him the beer upside down and punched a small hole in it with a folding knife. "I promise I'll help you find her in a sec if you do the same for me and Amber."

Jake sighed and accepted his fate. "Sure."

"Awesome!" Trevor flashed him a grin. "Cheers."

Jake endured the familiar experience of drinking a beer way too fast and then tossed the can into a nearly full recycling bin. Trevor immediately grabbed another beer to shotgun in quick succession, now with a few people cheering him on or joining in. Jake waited a minute before deciding to continue his search on his own.

He wasn't feeling the vibe. Even when he'd been in high school, this hadn't been his scene. He wondered if Kate would have ever bothered to go to a party like this if it wasn't for being invited by what amounted to her last remaining friend. He understood better why she'd wanted him to come along with her so badly.

He made his way up to the second floor, but he knew enough about how parties worked to guess what was going on in most of the rooms. It felt too much like a betrayal of his opinion and trust in Kate to even think for a moment that she'd be in one of them.

A laugh that he recognized drew his attention back downstairs. He saw Amber with her phone out, showing a video to a group of other teenagers.

He noted that one of them had definitely been among the group which had been tormenting Kate when he'd gone to pick her up from school on Thursday afternoon. He approached the group slowly, deliberately coming from an angle that put him behind Amber and out of her line of sight. He came close enough so he could see the phone screen and just barely hear the audio.

"Play it one more time!" said one of the girls.

"She seriously had no idea it was you?" asked a guy.

"None," said Amber. "She was completely fooled. I have multiple videos like this."

She hit play. Jake recognized Kate's room, though with enough differences to alert him to it being from a few years earlier. Kate came into frame wearing cat ears, with makeup whiskers on her cheeks and a black painted nose. She wore skimpy clothing and had a choker and leash on, which was more demeaning than accurate to the role play.

He felt his rage building as he watched her smiling and hopping around, doing cat-like stretches for "Daniel," her fictional boyfriend. She shook her butt and generally acted like a girl being silly and slutty for someone she loved. Jake saw red and pushed his way deeper into the group.

"You filmed this?" he snapped.

"She filmed this," said Amber. "And then sent it to Daniel, her boyfriend. He disappeared afterward. Strange. What? I didn't do anything, Jake."

"She thinks you're her friend," he said, baring his teeth as anger roiled through him.

"I am her friend," said Amber, haughtily. "She's lucky she has me as a friend. She's kind of weird and awkward, not to mention insanely immature. It's honestly a little bit her own fault that she gets bullied how she does."

"Fuck you," he said.

He snatched her phone away from her. Amber practically flew at him to try to get it back, but Jake was already moving. One of the windows looking out over the backyard and pool was open and he unceremoniously flung her phone out and into the water.

"You asshole!" she shouted. "I'll make you pay for that!"

"Where's Kate?" he snapped.

"How the fuck should I know? She left after like ten minutes."

Jake turned and headed for the door.

"Hey!" Trevor suddenly stepped in front of him. "What the fuck was that about."

"Get out of my face, Trevor."

The teenager pushed his shoulders. "Give me your phone! You fuck with my girl's shit, I fuck with yours!"

"Your loyalty's a little misplaced," said Jake. "She was grinding on some other dude just now."

He barely even saw Trevor's fist as it collided with his jaw, but the blow wasn't a hard one. He wiped blood off his lip.

"Are you eighteen?" he asked Trevor.

Trevor nodded his head. Jake punched him far harder than the blow he'd received and watched as he stumbled backward, grabbing for the wall.

"You psycho!" screamed Amber.

He pushed through the crowd, completely done with the party and situation. He needed to find Kate.

CHAPTER 24

It wasn't hard when Jake stopped to think about where Kate would be. It may have been four years since he'd spent much time with his little sister, but he distinctly remembered her favorite spot.

There was a small dog park on the edge of town that most people who weren't looking for a place for their canine to do their business avoided due to the poop rich grass and soil. At the center was a carefully curated circle of trees that anyone with enough patience could slip their way through to find a tiny clear patch at the center, free of animal feces and usually other people.

He remembered the first time Kate had showed him the spot when they'd been kids, dragging him along by the hand and insisting they have a secret base there. Jake had been more than happy to humor her with that much, though he'd stop short of playing the husband and wife game she'd tried to enlist him in. He chuckled to himself, wondering how they'd come so far without going anywhere at all.

"I heard you coming," came Kate's voice from inside as he walked up.

"My motorcycle has a pretty distinctive engine," he said. "Room for one more inside?"

"For you? Always."

It took him a minute to maneuver through the fence of branches and bushes and thin tree trunks. Kate was using her phone's light for illumination. She still had on the cute outfit he'd seen her depart in, tight jeans and a flirty blouse, though it looked so much more girlish with her sitting with her knees pulled in on the ground.

The missing bottle of wine that their mother had interrogated him about was next to her uncorked. Jake picked it up, more to test how much was left than to steal a sip. It was nearly empty.

"Did Mom send you looking for me?" she asked.

"Technically yes, but I came willingly." He took a seat next to her. "I went to the party."

She made an offended noise. "So when I ask you to go to a party with me, you refuse... and then show up after I've left? How is that fair?"

"Big brothers never play fair. You should know that by now."

She made a small noise of agreement. Jake wasn't sure how to broach the subject of Amber, what he'd discovered right before he'd left. Still, regardless whether he could find tactful words or do it gently, she deserved to know the truth.

"Your friend Amber... was part of your bullying," he said. "The fake boyfriend."

"I know," said Kate. "I knew it when I first realized what was happening, as soon as I realized that Daniel was just a bunch of instagram photos and empty promises. He appealed to me too much for her to not have been part of it, using my secrets against me. I don't know why Amber hated me so much back then, but I know that she did. She went along with it. She helped.

"I thought maybe, when she started reaching out to me again, that she felt guilty, or something. That she wanted to make up for it. Or maybe I'm just saying that. I had nobody, no friends, for so long, Jake. I guess I did rationalize it in my head. I was so lonely and, and, and..."

"Hey." He put an arm around her and pulled her closer. "It's okay."

"Maybe I am just a loser. Not just for being bullied, but for being so stupid. I knew that she had done such a terrible thing to me. But I was so starved and desperate for someone to just see me, and care about me. Isn't that what it means to be one of the losers? To just be so desperate that you pretend someone hasn't stabbed you in the back? That you pretend your own brother is, is...."

She broke into tears and Jake hugged her to him. He felt his heart tearing into pieces, slowly, like a band aid being ripped off in the most painful way. He wished he'd done more than just break the bitch's phone. Oh yeah.

"Want to know something funny?" he whispered.

She shook her head.

He told her anyway. "I threw Amber's phone in a pool."

Kate let out a small, reluctant chuckle through her tears.

"You want me to do it again once she buys a new one?"

She laughed a little more, and Jake reached to tickle her under the armpits like he used to when she was younger. She tried to tickle him back and his head brushed a sharp broken branch. He tipped at the wrong angle and she toppled over with him. She play wrestled atop him, but the tone of it almost immediately changed as their bodies came into contact at the middle.

"Jake..." She whispered against his ear and started kissing his neck. "I'm not... quite ready to go home yet."

Every muscle in his body, especially one in particular, screamed at him to flip her down underneath him and see how hard those jeans were to get off her. Except he was still her older brother. She'd drank an entire bottle of wine to the face at a hundred some odd pounds. She was emotional and, yes, probably struggling with a real, illicit attraction to him.

"Katie." He slid away from her a little and planted a chaste kiss on her head. "I love you so much. Enough to want you to protect you from everything. Including... this. Whatever the hell it is. Especially when you're this drunk."

"How is that fair?" she muttered, in the poutiest voice. She reached for her phone which still had the light on, and illuminated both their faces as she sat up. "Tonight has been awful, Jake. I just want my older brother to make it all better for me, and... what happened to your lip?"

"Ah." He touched it, noticing it wasn't bleeding much but definitely was a bit swollen. "Spencer punched me in the face."

"Who? Wait, you mean Trevor?"

"Whatever his name is. I punched him back after confirming he was eighteen."

Kate laughed and proceeded to dote on his face, not touching the lip, but tracing his jaw and cheek bone as though searching out the bruise. "You're seriously the coolest."

"I know."

"I feel like... you should at least get a reward, right?" Her hands slid lower until they were suddenly on his thigh. "Something to even the scale. You had to take a punch for me."

"It wasn't for you, Katie." He sighed, wanting to stop her but still summoning the willpower.

"Still..." She started tracing his cock with her fingers and he began to grow hard in record time. "Bet I could think of something that you'd like as a reward."

She leaned forward and low, coming to rest her chin on one of his legs. The idea of sweet little Katie's lips and mouth wrapped around his cock was almost enough to make him come just from that. He only wished they weren't in the dark, that he could see her cute little expression, embarrassed flushed cheeks, her look when he popped off and blew his load in her mouth, or all over her face.

He was a bastard of a brother, and she was still drunk.

"Have you ever thought about becoming a nun?" he asked, gently pushing her up and away from him by the shoulders.

"You're so mean, Jake!"

"Come on," he said. "It's almost one. I told Mom I was going to try to have you back by midnight."

She sighed, but followed along as he pushed out of the tree fence. Jake couldn't help but wonder if he'd come to regret being such a responsible older brother.

CHAPTER 25

"Jake?" called their mother, from the living room. "Is that you?"

"It is, and I found and rescued the sister."

"I'm fine, Mom," muttered Kate. "I just want to head to bed."

"Hold on." Rebecca came into the living room, looking like she'd been dozing on the couch and clad in a night robe. "I'm curious to hear if you know what happened to my wine, Kate. I'm missing a bottle."

Kate made a tired, grumbling noise. "No idea."

Jake shrugged, not about to snitch.

"Interesting," said his mom. "Well, I'll have to watch my wine cabinet more carefully in the future, regardless."

"Whatever you need to do, Mom."

"How was your night?"

"Fine."

Even in Kate's one syllable response, enough emotion leaked into the word to make it sound anything but fine. Rebecca sighed and walked over to her and gave her a hug.

"You smell like wine," she said.

"There was... some at the party," muttered Kate. "Jesus, Mom. It was a party, what do you expect?"

"Get some sleep, young lady. Thanks for bringing her home safe, Jake."

"No problem," he said.

He also went to bed, somewhat disoriented from his night. He stripped down to his boxers and stretched out under a single thin sheet. The scene with Kate in the trees played out over and over again with small changes, but he forced himself to not take advantage of her even in his mind. He still got an erection, but he didn't let himself fantasize, forced a boundary through sheer mental fortitude.

He was going to be living with her for the indefinite future. They'd both calm down after a week or two, and things would go back to how they'd been before he'd left, when she'd been his dorky fourteen-year-old sister who he'd so often been too busy to pay attention to. He frowned at the memory, knowing that casual disregard wasn't what Kate needed right now any more than an illicit drunken hookup.

Eventually, he did manage to get some sleep. He awoke midway through the night, unable to remember anything of his dream but sure it had related to sex, given how hard he was. Someone was opening the door to his room.

"Jake," whispered Kate. "I can't sleep."

She came into his room slowly, as if not wanting to wake him despite letting herself in. He sat up in bed, sighing and feeling the blood rushing to all the wrong places.

"Close the door," he whispered.

She did, doing it as slowly as possible to minimize the noise. The moon was out and he could see her clearly in silver light. Her hair was down, red locks loose and messy around her shoulders. She'd taken her glasses off and washed off her makeup, not that either made her any less beautiful. She had on a girlish pink nightgown and, judging from the way her nipples came to points under the fabric, no bra beneath it.

"I just don't want to be alone in my room tonight," she whispered. "Can I sleep in your bed with you? Just sleep. Seriously, nothing else."

There was an edge of carefully feigned innocence in her voice that made him chuckle quietly.

"You just don't give up, do you?" he said.

She shrugged. "Maybe I learned that from the horny guys at the party. I was only there for half an hour and two of them kept hitting on me, telling me how pretty and cool I am. I thought they were lying just to fuck with me, but then I realized they just wanted to fuck me."

He felt a flash of unnecessary jealousy. "Katie..."

"Then I remembered how hard you got when we were pretending," she whispered. "When you were helping me with my computer. And I wondered... if maybe you did, too."

"Come on," he said. "We shouldn't talk about this."

"Why not?" She climbed onto his bed and came closer to him on all fours, not seductively, but how she used to as a little girl. "What'll happen if we do?"

He felt suddenly annoyed at how dumb and rebellious she was being. He wondered what she'd do if he tested her, really pushed her until she reached her line and was the one suddenly drawing up a boundary. He wanted to kiss her, to do more than just that, and this time he didn't stop himself.

She blinked in surprise as his hand settled on her cheek. Her body seemed to sag forward into him as he kissed her. Her mouth moved hungrily against his. He laid her down on his bed, knowing exactly what he was doing, knowing that he'd lost his mind. He was too horny and too turned on by her to care.

"You can," she whispered. "It's okay. I remembered what you said about doing it with someone I loved when those guys were hitting on me."

"I don't think you heard what I meant," he muttered.

"I heard what you said."

She took his hand, kissed it, and pulled it to her breast. He'd been right — no bra underneath.

"You have to stay quiet." He rolled on top of her, kissing her neck and letting his boxer clad erection start to press between her thighs.

"I know," she whispered.

"I don't just mean tonight. Forever."

"I know!" she snapped, a little louder than he would have liked. "I'm not some naive little girl, Jake."

"You're not?" He let his hand palm her thigh, sliding under nightgown. "Are you sure about that?"

"I..." She trailed as Jake's fingers started gliding across her panties, identifying the hem, gently pulling it aside.

He didn't slide a finger into her right away, like he might have done out of eagerness with Estelle or Asa. Instead, he teased her a bit, indulging in her tiny little reactions. She was biting her lip, eyes fluttering. Her head was nodding with small movements that made it hard to tell whether she was urging him on or just twitching with pleasure.

He slid his fingertip across her clit and Kate gasped loud enough that Jake worried that he might have to slow down. She was clean shaven, and that in itself made him wonder about her intentions going to the party, how it might have gone had she not had another episode of bullying. She was also so wet that he couldn't help but wonder what it would feel like to fuck her.

"You said you were a virgin," he whispered. "But have you at least... you know. Made yourself come before?"

"...What?" Her breathing was crazy, and she was arching her hips up into his hand. "Jake... why would you ask me that?"

In truth, it was partly because he was curious about the remote and the vibrator. If he could do this much to her with two fingers and minimal effort, the Magic Pulse would reduce her to a writhing puddle. He slid his index and middle fingers into her, thumb gently caressing her clit.

"Oh fuck!" she moaned. "Jake!"

"Shhh! Quiet."

He curled his fingers inside her, watching her squirm and gasp, the moonlight reflecting in her eyes and illuminating her pale, petite thighs. Jake kissed her neck again and let his lips trace their way up to her ear.

"I've decided my goal is to make you come tonight, Katie," he whispered. "You deserve to. And somehow I don't think it will be very hard."

"Jake!" She shuddered, biting her lip to try to stifle a moan. "It feels so good!"

"Stay quiet," he said. "Or I'll stop."

It was a bold-faced lie. He had no intention of stopping until Kate was a gasping, sticky mess. He kissed her again on the neck, then the cheek, then the lips. She clumsily kissed him back, too pleasured to react quickly. He let his thumb tease her clit again and heard a faint, high pitched whine come from her body as all of her muscles tensed at once.

"Jake..." She bit her lip and shuddered. "I, I..."

"What?" He kept his voice teasing, almost condescending, and pulled the hand he was touching her with back. "What is it, Katie?"

She grabbed his wrist and made a pouting noise. "Meanie. I... think I'm close. Please."

"Please what?"

He gently pinched her nipple through her nightgown, and then pulled the garment up and over her head, leaving her naked save for her damp panties. She looked incredible in the moonlight, her perky breasts and pink nipples, her flat stomach and the slight curve of her hips. Jake's cock was aching in his boxers, almost painful.

"You're so fucking sexy, Katie," he whispered. He rolled on top of her and kissed one of her breasts, lips gliding over her nipple.

"Jake," she moaned. "I feel so... hot all over."

She bucked her hips up. Jake helped her out of her panties. She reached a hand down and played with the elastic of his boxers. He took those off too, heart pounding as he realized just how close to the line they were. A little voice in the back of his head begged him to stop, to pull back from defiling his little sister and changing their relationship irrevocably. A louder, eviler voice begged him to do it, to do her.

He meant to at least ask her if she was comfortable, give her one last chance to come to her senses and go back to her own bed. He meant to put a condom on, and to get up to make sure his door was locked. None of it materialized in the heat of the moment. Spreading Katie's thighs open, Jake let his cock tease at the entrance of her wet pussy for all of half a second before thrusting into forbidden bliss.

Kate gasped and Jake had to clamp a hand over her mouth to muffle the sound. She was so tight that it hurt in a good way, a sensation of her walls clenching around his cock and making every nerve ending sing with pleasure. He knew it was real and not a dream primarily from that, how wet and tight she was, how different her reactions were from how he'd imagined.

"Mmmm..." she moaned. "Fuck, Jake! Oh God!"

She bucked her hips up, urging him to take her harder before he'd even really started moving. He kissed her deeply and took the first real thrust into her sweet teenage cunt. There was no sensation of her hymen breaking, but he'd heard that wasn't unusual.

He had to be careful. He absolutely had to pull out. He pumped into her a few more times, hearing the telltale squeak of his bed underneath them. He had to be quiet, most of all.

Kate let out a fluttering moan. He shushed her and then kissed her and felt her breathing underneath him as their lips parted. She was panting and moaning with every thrust and he was quickly losing control of his own reactions, his own voice. He kissed her neck, then her collarbone, then her breasts.

He couldn't stop. Katie's pussy was incredible. She made a purring noise and rubbed her hands across his chest and shoulders. He remembered the stupid video of her Amber had been showing off, how into the kinky cat roleplay she'd gotten. His little sister was slutty in all the right ways. For her to be like this with him made him realize that she was being honest about how bad she wanted him.

Kate moaned his name and Jake silenced her with his hand this time, feeling the warm, wet heat of her breath, the suck of her pussy gliding along his cock. He drew his hand back and kissed her and slowed his pace, savoring the way her body felt. Kate whimpered and twitched with pleasure. Jake realized that she was close.

"Katie," he whispered against her neck.

"Jake!" She wrapped her arms tight around him, burying her face in his shoulder. It was both the cutest and sexiest thing that Jake had ever seen.

It might well have been her first ever orgasm, given her earlier reaction to him teasing her over the remote. Jake felt her pussy clamping down around him with tiny, insistent little clenches. He hugged her to him and sped up, hearing his bed squeaking and knowing it would betray him just as easily as her moaning. He couldn't stop himself from taking her hard, thrusting as deep as his cock would reach with each motion.

Kate arched her hips up, shaking and crying his name into his shoulder. Jake kissed her, feeling her pussy start to contract around him. He couldn't hold back any longer.

He came deep inside his little sister, filling her teenage pussy with his seed and pumping into her three more times. The pleasure was overwhelming, and he felt Kate still twitching through her own climax, which only made it better.

He couldn't remember if he'd ever made Estelle or Asa come like that, which told him that he probably hadn't. He kissed Kate softly on the lips and brushed a few messy strands of red hair out of her face.

They lay in his bed, a sweaty, naked pile of tangled limbs and hot breath. Jake finally felt his reason and sanity return to him, the guilt and the self-loathing both of what he'd done and how he'd done it. He'd straight up come inside his little sister, no condom, no sense. She snuggled into his side, still sticky from sex and breathing heavy.

"That's... how sex feels?" she whispered.

"Sometimes." He thought about it and realized he'd never had sex quite that good with his previous girlfriends. "Only when both people are really into it. Dammit, I should have pulled out."

"I can always get the morning after pill," whispered Kate. "Do you have condoms?"

"I do, but I don't think they'll do us much good now."

"Why not?" She furrowed her brow. "Aren't we going to go again?"

He noticed that she had one hand down between her thighs, touching herself right where he knew she'd still be sticky from his cum. It was insanely hot, and it made him think of both the video of her in her underwear and potentially her with the Magic Pulse. He would murder anyone who called his little sister a slut, but she definitely had a wild side.

"Give me a minute," he whispered, a smile sneaking onto his face.

"I could give you a minute along with... something else." She started leaving a trail of kisses down his chest, across his stomach.

Jake let out a low groan and felt his arousal stirring back to life at record pace. He wondered just how depraved Katie might end up being if this was her first experience of sex, already so deep in taboo territory. He'd be the first to find out. Her kisses ran down his thigh, and he saw her look up at him and meet his gaze as she licked his cock, which was still sticky from minutes earlier.

"Teach me how to do this?" she whispered.

"Sure." He chuckled, wondering how much experience he really had. Asa had hated blowjobs and Estelle had only given him them on special occasions. "Kiss the tip to start. You can use your hands along with your mouth."

Kate licked his shaft and kissed the tip, eyes flicking back and forth between him and his member as though looking for approval. Jake petted her hair, loving the feel of it through his fingers. She took the tip of his cock into her mouth and began sucking, swirling her tongue around it.

He let his fingers gently wrap through her hair near the roots and started guiding her motions. Kate seemed to enjoy it and started moving her head a little faster, letting his cock push deeper and deeper into her mouth. He felt the tip touch the back of her throat and almost let out a grunt as he pulled back.

The sight of his sweet little sister with her lips wrapped around his cock made what they were doing feel dirty and wrong all over again, even more than it had before when he'd been resisting.

He wondered how their mother would react if she ever found out, how he would ever be able to look her in the eye or have her trust again. Kate moaned and bobbed her head a little faster, sucking his cock like she was getting something of her own out of it.

"Katie," he whispered. "Fuck, Katie."

He was already getting close. He let his fingers trail down from her hair. Kate kept going at that same pace, putting on a performance of a blowjob that gave him that tingling, imminent feeling. Kate seemed to notice his pleasure and stopped, pulling her mouth off his tool with a lewd popping noise.

"Is this alright?" A bead of pre-cum or saliva glistened on her lower lip.

"Perfect," he muttered. "But do you know what would be even better?"

She shook her head, the motion somehow both girlish and guileless. He fondled one of her tits and pulled her upward by the arm, kissing her once before flipping her down underneath him.

"Roll over," he whispered.

"Oh fuck!" she moaned. "Jake!"

She did exactly what he asked and pushed her butt up into the air, wiggling it with needy motions. Jake leaned over her, hands drawn to her pert little breasts once more. He smoothed her hair out of the way of her neck and kissed her.

"Remember to stay quiet," he whispered.

"I am staying quiet!" she hissed, in a pouty voice. "And I'm ready. Do it, Jake. Fuck me hard."

He groaned, wondering if he'd ever heard her swear so many times before. She had a dirty mouth. Dirty and good at sucking cock. He let his erection press into the wet folds of her pussy, taking her by the waist as he pushed his hips forward for the first solid thrust.

Kate let out a tiny, needy moan and pressed her butt back into him. Jake kept his motions slow to start, his hands trailing across her stomach, across her shoulders, back around to her breasts. She was so perfect, a cute, sexy little sister who could give him so much pleasure. Illicit pleasure. Secret pleasure. He sped up, pumping into her from behind fast enough for the clap of their bodies to join the squeaking of the bed.

Kate at least had the ability to bury her face in the pillow to muffle her own sounds of pleasure. Jake couldn't stop himself from feeling possessive, protective, even loving as the events of the party flashed back through his mind. He didn't want anyone else ever to touch Katie like this. She was his. His little sister. His lover. His toy.

"Jake!" moaned Kate into the pillow. "Fuck! More! More!"

He gave one of her buttocks a soft slap and a shudder of pleasure ran through her. He sped up, fucking her hard enough for her body to start jerking forward from the impact of their motions. Kate braced herself against the headboard, which helped her stay in position but doubled the noise of the bed. Jake spanked her again and watched her butt shake a little from the impact.

"Meanie," she moaned.

"You like it," he whispered.

"I love it, Jake." She waggled her butt for him, glancing over her shoulder. "I'm a dirty girl."

She reached her hand back between her thighs, rubbing at her clit. Jake sped up again, thrusting into her faster and harder, worried the noise of the bed would betray them but too turned on to care. Katie was moaning his name, calling him a meanie, gasping and moaning and driving him crazy. He was about to come again.

"Katie," he moaned. "Fuck!"

"Jake!"

He was about to come, and it was only then that he remembered that he'd forgotten to put a condom on again. His mind was quick to rationalize. He had already come in her once that night. What difference would twice, or even three times make? Four? He sped up and heard Kate let out a cry of pleasure that bit off as she muffled herself with the pillow.

He couldn't stop himself. Jake came a second time inside his little sister, claiming her pussy with his seed. Kate writhed as her own orgasm ran its course, eyes fluttering, body collapsing forward. He leaned over her with his cock still sheathed in her cunt, planting gentle and loving kisses on her shoulder and cheek.

"So... that's why sex is such a big deal," she whispered.

Jake chuckled and pulled out of her, wrapping her in hug. "Yeah. Though in my experience, it's usually not that good."

"Mmm." Kate smiled sleepily at him. "So does that mean I'm good at it?"

"You're a natural, Katie."

"Yay."

"A natural slut." He gave her another soft spank.

"Hey!" She hit him with the pillow. "Don't be a jerk!"

"I'm just teasing you." He kissed her on the lips. "I now have a range of new ways to tease you, Katie."

"Take it back."

"I meant it as a compliment. You're my little slut." He touched her chin and turned her head so they were looking into each others eyes. "And I love you. So much."

"I love you, too."

CHAPTER 26

Jake couldn't bear to kick Kate out of his bed immediately. He let her sleep cuddled up with him, though he had the sense to set an early alarm for 4 AM. It went off before he'd fallen asleep himself, which made sense, giving how much time they'd spent fucking.

"Katie," he whispered. "You have to go back to your room."

"I don't want to," she muttered.

He kissed her forehead. "You have to. We have to be careful. So careful. Mom or Jaimie can never catch us waking up together."

"They won't catch us," whispered Kate. "As long as you can keep from molesting me when we're right in front of them."

"I'll save that for behind closed doors," he whispered, with a smile. "Seriously, though, Katie."

"They aren't going to assume that we're fooling around with each other solely based off us spending a lot of time together. Think about how much of a leap in logic that would be. Not everybody has a mind as dirty as yours, Jake."

She reached over and touched his cock. He felt himself getting hard instantly. It was still dark out his window, but there was no way they could risk it at a time when his mother or Jaimie could theoretically wake up early and be up for the rest of the morning.

"You have to go back to your room, Katie," he whispered again.

"What's this?"

He thought she was talking about his cock in a coy, dirty way until he realized she'd found the remote on his bed stand. Jake chuckled, wondering how to explain.

"I found that in the couch cushions downstairs," he said. "It's a vibrator remote. A sex toy."

He watched her reaction carefully, but he was already ninety nine percent sure she wasn't the owner of the Magic Pulse.

"Gross," she muttered. "Doesn't that mean someone was using it on the couch?"

"It means either Jaimie or Mom was using it on the couch," he said.

"Even grosser!"

He nodded, but gross wasn't exactly the word he would have used. He felt his arousal stirring with even more ferocity than previously, as though crossing the line with Kate had primed him to continue his investigation with new vigor.

"Still though," he said. "Aren't you curious?"

"Maybe a little." She shrugged, her hand wandering back to his cock. "It doesn't make sense, though. How would the remote get lost in the first place?"

"What do you mean?" He felt himself getting far too turned on by her touch.

"Isn't the vibrator useless without the remote?"

"Obviously."

"So obviously whoever used it would go looking for the remote when they realized they didn't have it," said Kate. "Or they used it so recently that they haven't realized it's missing yet."

Jake nodded slowly. "Insights like that are why I'm glad you're my sister."

"Is that the only reason?" She took his cock in both hands and started to shift closer toward him for a kiss, for maybe more.

The sound of music playing from Jaimie's room made them both freeze. Jake waited a few seconds and then gave Kate a serious look.

"How about we continue this conversation tomorrow night?" he asked. "Once everyone has gone to bed."

"I bet we could find time during the day," she whispered. "It's Sunday. Mom will be out shopping and Jaimie is always out doing Jaimie stuff."

"We'll see."

Kate stroked his cock and kissed him once. "Or we could head out into town. See a movie. Find somewhere private."

She kissed him again, deeper this time. Jake touched her shoulders and reluctantly but firmly pushed her back.

"You need to get back to your room before Jaimie finishes getting up," he said.

"I'm going, I'm going." She climbed out of his bed and started gathering her clothes. "Goodnight, Jake. And good morning. Love you."

"Love you too."

He gave a small pat on the butt to encourage her to move faster. Kate giggled and blew him a kiss as she silently slipped out the door.

THANKS FOR READING

If you enjoyed this book, I encourage you to leave a review on Amazon. It's really a huge help! If you're interested in hearing about my books as soon as they're published, either follow me on my Amazon author page or visit www.anyamerchant.com.

Household Obsession

Made in United States
Troutdale, OR
12/30/2024